FIRST Lady OR NOT

GABRIELLE BEASLEY

Published by
Genesis Productions
PO Box 21102
Bedford, TX 76095

ISBN-13 978-1-7324378-0-7 (print)

ISBN-13 978-1-7324378-1-4 (ebook)

Printed in the United States of America.

Design by Karie Williams.

For information about special discounts for bulk purchasing,
please email genesistheater@gmail.com.

Acknowledgements

I have to first thank my Lord and Savior, Jesus Christ, for ordering my steps and loving me when I didn't love myself. Thank you for blessing me with my gift of writing; it's my best form of expression.

I want to acknowledge those who played a part in bringing "First Lady or Not" to life: Ericka Araujo, Shandalyn Hicks, Reginald and Natoyia Jyles, Revonne Rallings-Law, Kenneisha Thompson, and Latisha Tryon. Thank you all so much for supporting this project.

I would also like to thank my family and friends for your love and support. Every word of encouragement, piece of advice given, and nudge to finish this book has been priceless. Words can't truly express my love and gratitude to each and every one of you.

Finally, I would like to thank my cousin, Cassandra Bassett, for all of your life lessons and great conversations. Through those conversations "First Lady or Not" was born.

Prologue

Crystal swung and kicked with all of her might as two male techs used their strength to hold her down. She had even resorted to spitting, but her efforts were no match.

"Crystal, if you ever want to get out of here, you're going to have to take your meds. Fighting is only going to prolong your stay."

Crystal refused to acknowledge the nurse's words whether they were right or not. She only had a little bit of dignity left. Willingly taking the medicine meant the doctor's diagnosis was true. Crystal refused to admit that she suffered from chronic depression.

Just yesterday she'd watched a woman have a fight with herself. The lady had literally clawed at her skin until her pink flesh was exposed. She wasn't sure who'd won the fight, but Crystal knew the outcome hadn't been pleasant either.

What she did know was that she wasn't like the rest of the patients in the psych ward. She was able bodied and she didn't need medication to function. She would never forgive her mother for allowing them to bring her here. She shouldn't be surprised, though. Her mother never had her best interest at heart. Crystal was snatched from her thoughts with the nurse's next words.

"You've forced my hand, Crystal. I'm going to have to administer your meds through IV."

"I'm not crazy." Crystal could only muster a weak verbal protest as her body surrendered to the medicine being pushed through her veins.

"Try and relax. In the next few moments, you're about to have the best sleep of your life."

Her vision began to go out of focus as sleep took her body captive. Crystal thought back to how she had arrived at this season in her life. She always knew that men would get her in trouble, but never in her life did she think her infatuation for them would take her down such a dark path.

Unable to fight any longer, Crystal gave in to the sleep that impatiently waited on her, praying that when she woke up, she'd no longer be confined to the psych ward and life would return to normal.

Chapter 1

Crystal stared at herself in the gold-framed mirror hanging on her living room wall. She had just finished applying the new lipstick, Heroine, that she'd purchased from the MAC cosmetics store. The mirror was the only thing she had left from her grandmother. Lord knows she missed that woman dearly. Her grandmother had been her haven. Many times she'd offered Crystal a warm bed when her mother had failed to keep the lights on. She could talk to her grandmother endlessly about anything.

Crystal hadn't been the same since she died six years ago. There was a void in her heart that nothing or no one would ever be able to fill. That was the main reason why the mirror had traveled everywhere she'd been since she'd received it. The mirror would always be a part of the décor of her home. She made it match, rather indifferent, to whether it did or didn't.

The mirror wasn't just an heirloom that had been passed down to her. No, it meant much more than that. Her grandmother always wanted Crystal to be able to see who she really was. Her grandmother often told her she was beautiful, but her grandmother wasn't focused on just the physical. Crystal could still hear her grandmother saying, "Until, you learn who you really are, you'll never know your worth. You have to be more than pretty to make it in this world, girl."

Crystal knew the advice her grandmother had given her was true. Which is why guilt tugged at her as she smoothed the few flyaway hairs of her freshly styled hair. There were many days she struggled to see past her looks. She had never been told that she was smart or funny, only pretty. Crystal's beauty had allowed her to be in the company of some of the most eligible bachelors. She didn't know who she would be if she didn't have her good looks. Oftentimes that scared her, but she'd never showed her fear. Crystal held her head so high, most people believed she lived in a perfect world, with the best of everything. She was great at putting on facades. Her mother, Essie, had taught her that skill well.

But for now, the mirror simply reflected her beautiful face as she modeled the ruby red hat that she'd just brought from a boutique in downtown Dallas. The hat was more expensive than she could afford, but the look on Marcus's face when he saw her in it would be well worth the price. He was on his way over, and she wanted the hat to be the first thing seen when she opened the door. She would have preferred to model the hat in nothing but her birthday suit, but her daughters would be home soon, so for now that wasn't an option.

Marcus was her current boyfriend; soon-to-be husband, and the love of her life. He completed her world by simply being in it. Marcus was sexy; Crystal would often catch herself just staring at him. He was six-five and pure chocolate, just like Crystal liked her men. Marcus worked out five days of the week and his chiseled body proved his dedication to the gym. His soft eyes and his million-dollar smile were just a bonus. The best part of it all was that Marcus was a man of God. He was currently the co-pastor of Freewill Baptist. That's where she had met him two years ago, and she couldn't be happier. At the time, she didn't like the direction her church, Mountain View Baptist, was headed. She'd decided to visit some different churches in her local area to find a new church home.

Freewill Baptist was welcoming enough, but when Pastor Marcus Powers stepped into the pulpit, he had her undivided attention. Just like his last name, Marcus was a man of power, and he knew how to make things happen. The prayer he prayed that morning gave Crystal goose-bumps. After service, she went to introduce herself and the rest was history. That one introduction turned into Crystal attending Bible study, phone calls, and then lunch and dinner dates. She would soon be Marcus Power's first lady. Being a first lady had been her dream since she was a little girl, and now it was about to be reality.

Every first lady that Crystal had ever known was beautiful, well dressed and adored by the congregation. Other than her grandmother, she hadn't been adored by anyone. Growing up, girls were jealous of Crystal because of her good looks, so friends hadn't come easy.

To Crystal, being a first lady meant that she had arrived in stature. Most importantly she would be surrounded with the love she'd longed for her entire life. Marriage to Marcus would improve her life financially as well. She would be able to provide more for her daughters. Marcus promised to give her all that and more, once he got everything lined up. Being a co-pastor of a church was more than a full-time job. Their time together was often limited. At times the limitation of his schedule would really frustrate Crystal.

She knew their love was real and worth the wait. She thanked God every day for bringing Marcus into her life. He was the missing piece to her puzzle. Now, if she could only get her two daughters Lesley and Aisha to see things the same way. Marcus would be their stepfather soon, and she didn't want anything coming between her and Marcus's union.

There was a soft knocking at the door.

"There's my baby right there." Crystal said as she secured her new hat on her head. "Wait until Marcus sees me."

Crystal sashayed to the door as if she had an audience of men. She opened the door and tried to play it cool, but what stood before her was a true work of art. Crystal tried to hide her smile, but she never could with Marcus.

"Hey, baby." She cooed.

"Hey, yourself." Marcus made his way into the house and sat on Crystal's plush white sofa.

Crystal couldn't hide her disappointment. Marcus didn't greet her with a hug or a kiss, and he didn't even mention her new hat. They hadn't seen each other in two weeks. She was hoping he would show a little more enthusiasm about seeing her after all this time.

His facial expression told Crystal he had a lot on his mind.

"Is that how you greet your future wife?" Crystal joked, trying to lighten the mood.

"I'm sorry… I'm just stressed."

Crystal hated to see her man like this, and she would do or be whatever he needed to make him happy.

"What's up babe?" Crystal asked as she sat next to Marcus.

"I'm in a bind. Crystal and I really need your help."

"Whatever it is, Marcus, we'll get through this together." Crystal said as she began to massage Marcus's hand.

"I'm glad to hear you say that."

Crystal's heart began to race with those words. Since they started dating two years ago, Marcus had never been vulnerable with her. She'd always wanted him to be, but she figured that men just didn't show that side of themselves.

"I'm here, baby."

Crystal watched the folds in Marcus's forehead begin to disappear as the tension escaped his body.

"I need a loan."

"A loan, Marcus? You still owe me five hundred dollars from the last loan." Trying to hide her sarcasm and be the supportive girlfriend didn't go over well, but it seemed she'd been helping Marcus a lot financially, lately.

"You're keeping score for what you do for me? I thought we were better than that."

Crystal didn't want to argue with Marcus and she sure didn't want him questioning her loyalty. She tried taking a hold of his hand to reassure him that her loyalty was with him, but the way he snatched it away told her that he wasn't feeling it.

"Marcus, please don't be like that. You know I got your back. It's just... I don't think you realize that I'm a single parent who receives no child support."

"Which is all the reason why you should know that I wouldn't ask you unless I really need it."

"You're putting me between a rock and a hard place... I honestly can't afford to do this."

"Well, I guess that's my answer."

Watching him walk towards the door, Crystal felt herself relent to his request.

"What do you need the money for, Marcus? You work for a

church, I'm sure that the congregation will raise an offering for you."

Her words stopped him in his tracks, but he wouldn't turn and look at her. There was something he wasn't saying, and she wanted the truth before she gave him anything.

"There's some random woman at the church spreading rumors about being pregnant by me, but baby I swear none of it is true. Anyway, if I don't pay for the abortion she's going to come forth to the congregation."

Crystal couldn't believe the words that she was hearing. Marcus had just indirectly told her that he had been cheating on her. He'd distanced himself lately, and Crystal had told herself that he was just busy with work. Now, her worst fear had come to light. She felt humiliated, not only with the new discovery, but because she knew in her heart that she wasn't ready to let him go. Who would ever love her like Co-Pastor Marcus Powers? She wasn't ready to give up on them. She had to prove to him that she was down no matter what. Crystal knew what she had to do.

"How much do you need?" Crystal asked as she grabbed her purse from the sofa table.

"Only three hundred dollars."

"I hope you know you're taking from my kids' mouths", Crystal said as she handed Marcus the check.

"That's why I love you so much." Marcus said as he pulled Crystal into his arms.

Taking in the scent of his cologne, Crystal relished the moment. His arms are where she belonged.

"Ma, where you at?"

Crystal cringed because her perfect moment was over. The tightness in Marcus's body let her know that he felt the same way too. Crystal had hoped that Marcus would be long gone before her eldest daughter got home. Lesley and Marcus didn't see eye to eye, and it was always ugly when the two were in the same space.

"Ma, where are you?"

"I'm in the living room."

"Ma, are you cooking today?"

"I'm doing well, Lesley. How are you? It would be nice to be acknowledged before being bombarded with questions."

"Sorry, but are you cooking today? I'm starving."

Crystal watched Lesley's demeanor change when she realized that she and Crystal weren't alone.

"Why does he always have to be here?"

"Lesley, you will respect my guest."

"Why? He doesn't respect you."

"It's good to see you again, Lesley." Marcus said to Lesley.

Crystal knew Marcus was only trying to keep the peace for her sake. She hated to admit that Marcus didn't like Lesley, he only tolerated her.

"Well, it's never good to see you," Lesley threw back at Marcus.

"Crystal, I'm going to get out of here. Thanks again for all your help." As he kissed Crystal on the cheek he whispered, "I'm going to pray for you because you got your hands full with Lesley."

"I tell her the same thing about you, Marcus! And if you don't want me to hear you, try working on your whispering skills." Lesley shot back.

"I'll handle Lesley," Crystal said.

Marcus left without saying another word. She made a mental note to make sure he knew to not talk against her daughter ever again. Lesley may have been a headache, but she was her headache and she wouldn't allow anybody else talking bad about her.

"Lesley, whether you want to accept it or not, Marcus is a part of my life and will be officially a part of this family very soon. I suggest you get your attitude in check."

"Well, are you cooking today? I'm starving."

Lesley tossed Crystal's words aside like an old rag, which only infuriated Crystal all the more. Lesley had completely ignored what Crystal had just said.

"I'm cooking later. If you're hungry, go eat a bowl of cereal until dinner is ready."

"Okay. I also need money for my senior trip."

"Where are y'all going and how much do you need?"

"We're going to Disney World and it's six hundred dollars per person."

"Disney World sounds like so much fun, but I'm sorry, Lesley. I don't have an extra six hundred dollars in my budget to give. I will try my best to make it happen. When do you need it?"

Lesley let her backpack slide down her arm and hit the floor. There was a big thud that caused Crystal to give her daughter a long hard look over. Lesley was beautiful, the splitting image of herself minus seventeen years. Actually, Lesley was far more beautiful than Crystal had ever been. The dark green swing dress that Lesley wore accented her figured quite nicely. The gold cross necklace that Essie had given her for her sixteenth birthday added a nice touch to Lesley's looks. Crystal loved the fact that her daughter was so creative with her style of dress. She never tried to conform to the style of the time and she'd never chased labels.

"Les, I just don't have that kind of money lying around."

"Ma, are you serious? This is my senior trip we're talking about. You're not even going to try to come up with the money?"

"I just said I would try my best. I don't get overtime at the church and I don't have any other sources of income."

"I wonder how many times you've saved Marcus when he's in a bind."

"Lesley, what did you say?"

"We know, Ma. How many times have we been without lights, water and even food for his sake? I thought a man was supposed to provide for his woman, not the other way around. Why can't you get the money from him? I'm sure he has to owe you thousands of dollars?"

Crystal could feel her blood pressure rise instantly. The throbbing at her left temple was causing her to become nauseated. High blood pressure did run in her family, and she knew she would need to see a doctor soon. That would have to wait for another day. Right now she had to set her daughter straight. Who did Lesley think she was to question her relationship?

"Lesley, I suggest you stay in a child's place. You're too young to understand my relationship with Marcus."

"No Ma, I understand perfectly well. You're taking care of a man who's already married, and we suffer because of it. You make good money, but we can never tell because Marcus gets most of it."

Tears started to form in Lesley's eyes, and it killed Crystal to see the pain her daughter was in, but Crystal couldn't console her daughter right now. Consoling her meant Lesley was right, and her pride couldn't admit that, even to make her child feel better.

"When will you get that he isn't in love with you and he's only using you? I may only be a child, but I do understand that. I'm going on my senior trip, with or without your help. You've cheated us enough. I won't let you take this from me!"

Reaching for her bag, Lesley stormed out of the house. She slammed the door so hard it caused Crystal's grandmother's mirror to shift. Had the mirror fallen and broken, Crystal would've been devastated. Thankful the mirror was okay, Crystal directed her focus on the argument she and Lesley had just had. They've had some bad ones, but never had Lesley been so disrespectful. How did she know that she had lent Marcus money?

Her mother Essie had to be the culprit. Essie despised Marcus more than Lesley did. Enough was enough. She had no right trying to turn her children against her by spreading lies.

Chapter 2

Crystal stood outside her mother's two-story brick Dallas home. The house held four bedrooms and a two-car garage. The home was decorated beautifully. It was accented with vaulted ceilings, chandeliers in just about every room, stainless steel appliances, and marble floors. It was a far reach from how Crystal grew up. They had always lived in one-bedroom apartments throughout her childhood. Crystal hadn't had her own bedroom until she'd moved out on her own.

Had her mother been doing her best to keep a roof over their heads, Crystal would have been more understanding. Unfortunately that hadn't been the case. Essie loved to be in the company of men and would do whatever it took to keep them in her life; oftentimes, that meant she would pay men to keep them around. Which is why Crystal couldn't understand the audacity of Essie's decision to go blab her business to her girls. Essie had freely given money to men who had no potential to be anything more than lovers.

The more Crystal thought about it, the more she burned with anger. Pellets of sweat formed on her nose and it had nothing to do with the Texas heat. She couldn't believe her mother would go that far and spread her personal business with her children. Then she thought about it; Essie had always made it her business to make Crystal's life hell. Why would this time be any different?

Boom! Boom! Boom! Crystal banged on her mother's front door so hard she felt the pain radiate from her fist down to her elbow. She completely disregarded the doorbell on purpose. Crystal wanted to make sure her mother felt every bit of her wrath.

"Just a minute! Just a minute!"

Crystal could hear her mother's frustration. Essie was preparing herself to tear into whoever was on the other side of the door. Crystal didn't care one bit. She welcomed the tongue-lashing. This way she wouldn't feel so bad about disrespecting her mother.

"This better be an emergency! Why are you knocking at my door like a bat out of hell?" Essie fired as soon as she swung the door open.

Crystal stormed past Essie without saying a word.

"Crystal, I asked you a question. Why are you knocking on my door like you're crazy? Is there an emergency of some kind?"

"Yes. My children are always an emergency."

"Oh my God, is something wrong with Lesley and Aisha?"

"You're what's the matter with them, Essie. The foolery stops today." Crystal demanded as she dropped onto one of the tan barstools at the kitchen counter.

"Crystal, what are you talking about?"

"I don't understand why you're so against my relationship with Marcus. Why would you tell Lesley that I've let Marcus borrow money? She's a child. What happens in my dating life is none of her business."

The eruption of laughter from Essie was not the response that Crystal hoped to receive.

"What's funny? This is serious. Lesley and I had the worst fight ever. All because of your lies."

"How dare you charge your way into my home playing the good mother? You've always had a way of seeing things differently when it benefits you."

"Essie, what are you talking about?"

Crystal watched as Essie sashayed to the other side of the counter and took a sip of her coffee.

"Crystal, let's be truthful here. When you let someone borrow money, there's the intention from them to pay you back. How many times has Marcus paid you back in the two years that you've been seeing him? None? I'm sure he promises he will, but when it's time to pay, he always has an excuse. Don't even try to deny it."

"Why does my happiness always have to be sacrificed? I never once tried to block your happiness. Why is it so hard for you to return the favor?"

"Crystal, nobody is trying to block your happiness. That man is only using you and you're the only one who refuses to see it."

"Whether you're willing to accept it or not, he's my man and your future son-in-law."

"Ha! As long as he's another woman's husband, he'll never be your man."

Crystal could feel the burn in her throat as she fought to hold back tears. To say Essie's words hurt would be an understatement. Yes, Marcus was married, but he was truly unhappy with his marriage. He constantly told Crystal how his wife didn't make him feel as good as she did. He spent every free moment that he could with her, and he often said, if it wasn't for his children he would have left a long time ago. Crystal understood the importance of children having both parents around. She often felt there was a piece of her missing because she'd never met her father.

"Essie, I don't expect you to understand our relationship because you've always paid your men to stay around. You're just jealous that I have someone in my life that truly loves me. I'm not going to keep going back and forth with you, but as I said before stop feeding my kids lies."

Crystal knew her tone wouldn't sit well with Essie. One thing her mother didn't tolerate was a disrespectful child, no matter what the age. Bending over the countertop, Essie put her face so close to Crystal's that Crystal could smell the hazelnut from the coffee on Essie's breath.

"As long as you're always in my pockets for money, you have no personal business. And don't ever come into my house where I pay the bills and make any demands."

Crystal knew it was no arguing with her mother. She was so set in her ways. Once she made her mind up about something there was no turning back. Crystal hated to admit that was one characteristic that they both shared. Grabbing her purse from the counter, she rose to leave. She felt so unsettled about the way she was leaving, without Essie having an understanding on where she stood in regards to her children or Marcus. Crystal knew she wasn't the perfect parent by far, but anything or anyone trying to sabotage her relationship with her children had to go, and that included her mother.

"Make this the last time you volunteer my business to my kids. If you can't respect that, I'll make it so you'll never see them again."

"Your threats don't scare me. As long as Marcus is in your life, you'll always need me."

Chapter 3

Two weeks had passed since Crystal's fight with Essie. She had tried to block out Essie's hurtful words. She would be lying to herself if she didn't admit Essie's words had spoken volumes, especially the ones about her and Marcus. The fact that she hadn't talked to Marcus since she'd loaned him the money only added to her insecurities. She'd tried to call him several times, and with each call he'd sent her straight to voicemail. That wasn't like Marcus. Whenever he missed her call or was too busy to talk, he always called her back. She had become worried, but since their relationship was a secret, she had to be careful in the manner of how she questioned his whereabouts. Fortunately, today was Friday, and she would only have to wait two more days to see him. Once their relationship had become serious, Marcus had decided it be best that she stopped attending Freewill, so they wouldn't complicate things. Crystal still didn't understand Marcus's logic, but she wanted their relationship to work, so she went with it. She knew Marcus would be upset about going against his wishes, but she didn't care. Crystal couldn't wait any longer to see him.

"Hey Crystal, don't forget I need that report by two."

Crystal was so deep in thought that she hadn't heard Pastor Davis enter her office.

"Crystal?"

Snapping back from her thoughts, Crystal whirled around in her chair to face Pastor Davis. His handsome features and athletic build were definitely a sight for sore eyes. Crystal was more biased toward darker-skinned men, but she would be willing to bend for Pastor Davis's smooth ivory skin. He had eyes the color of honey, which were mesmerizing. Rumor had it that many women had tried to get in the sheets with Pastor Davis, but he only had eyes for his wife. Everyone knew that he adored his first lady dearly. She was one blessed woman.

"I'm so sorry, Pastor Davis, my mind was somewhere else. I'll definitely have the report ready by then. Actually, it will be ready within the next fifteen minutes."

"Thanks, Crystal. You can just bring it to my office when you're finished. Are you doing okay today?"

"Yes, Pastor."

Crystal returned to her work. Normally she was two steps ahead of Pastor Davis, but not hearing from Marcus had really thrown her off her game.

"Excuse me, Crystal?"

Hearing that sweet voice instantly made Crystal's lips turn up. It was Mrs. Parsons, one of the most faithful volunteers at New Hope. Mrs. Parsons and her husband had been over the marriage ministry for the last five years. Crystal couldn't think of a better couple to teach the class. The pair had been married for over sixty years. Crystal could still see their passion when the two looked at each other and they still held hands. It's as if they were still in the honeymoon stage after all these years.

Rising from her seat, Crystal walked around her desk to hug Mrs. Parsons.

"Mrs. Parsons, how are you?"

"I'm well and yourself?"

"I'm good, just very busy. What brings you by the office today?"

"Well, my husband and I have to go out of town last minute, and we're supposed to be passing out flyers this Sunday for the marriage conference coming up in a few weeks. I wanted to see if there was any way you could pass the flyers out for us?

Crystal could feel her disappointment, but she didn't want it to show. Passing out the flyers meant she wouldn't be able to visit Freewill this Sunday. But she couldn't say, "no" to Mrs. Parsons. She loved everything the woman stood for and she had always been extremely kind to Crystal and her girls.

"Sure. You can leave the flyers in the sanctuary and I'll make sure they get passed out."

"Thank you so much. I'll have my husband bring the box inside."

Crystal waited for Mrs. Parsons to leave her office before she returned to her seat. She couldn't help but wonder if she and Marcus could have a relationship like Mr. and Mrs. Parsons. It was truly something that she longed for, but Crystal knew relationships like theirs were one in a million.

Crystal glanced at the clock and realized fifteen minutes had passed. She needed to get the expense report to Pastor Davis. She printed out the report and walked to the printer, which was located right next to Pastor Davis's office. His back faced the door, but by his tone, Crystal could tell he was having a heated conversation.

Unable to contain her nosiness, she began to eavesdrop. She'd worked with Pastor Davis for two years and had never seen him this irritated. He'd always been a mild-mannered man.

"Yes, Mary. I'm here at the office. You know my role as senior pastor keeps me away from home more than I would like to be. Our family is the most important thing to me. How could you say I don't care? Look, I'll be home early today. I promise we can talk about this then. I really need to get ready for my board meeting today and I still need to look over the report Crystal prepared for me. Yes, Crystal is here…she's my assistant. Mary don't you go there! I'll see you when I get home. Goodbye."

Crystal couldn't believe what she had just heard. It looked like there was trouble in paradise. Mrs. Davis was no fool. She knew that there were women ready and willing to be in her position. She was fighting for her family, and Crystal didn't blame her one bit.

"Excuse me, Pastor. I have that report you needed."

He wore a frown and Crystal didn't like seeing her boss so out of character.

"Pastor, are you okay? You seem upset?"

"I'm fine."

Taking a few steps at a time, Crystal hesitated to enter his office. Never seeing him so upset, Crystal wasn't for sure what angle to come at him, but curiosity had gotten the best of her and she needed to confirm what she thought she heard.

"Pastor, just pray about it. God is in control."

"Thanks, Crystal. It's a blessing to have good God-fearing people around. Even pastors need to be encouraged. People seem to forget that."

"I completely understand. May I ask you something, sir?"

"Sure."

"I honestly wasn't trying to eavesdrop. When I was at the printer I heard you on the phone. Was your wife accusing us of having an affair?"

"Crystal, I'm not for sure what my wife was doing."

Crystal didn't know how to respond. She could definitely feel the uneasiness in the room she had just created. Thankful she remembered the report she'd been holding.

"Well, here's your report. I'm going to wrap up my work, so I can be caught up before five. If you need anything, just let me know."

"Thanks, Crystal."

As Crystal walked back to her office, she could hear the desk phone ringing. She did a light sprint to the phone so she wouldn't miss the call. "Ouch!" Crystal had stomped her pinkie toe on the corner of the desk. Her entire foot instantly radiated with pain.

"New Hope Church, this is Crystal. How may I help you?"

"Hey, Crystal. You aren't too busy are you? I hate bothering you at work."

""Oh hey, Yolanda. Actually, I'm trying to clear my desk, so I can be out of here on time."

"Okay. I wanted to come by the house this evening. I haven't seen you or my nieces in a while. We need to catch up."

"Ain't that the truth? Come on by, I'll be there no later than six."

"Okay, hun. See you soon."

"Goodbye."

Crystal hung the receiver up and just sat in silence while she massaged her aching foot. Today had definitely been a string of strange events. If anybody could help her make sense of it all, it would be her best friend Yolanda. Yolanda had been there for Crystal's lowest and highest moments in life, and she never regretted asking her for advice.

Chapter 4

Crystal stood in the doorway in disbelief. The living room looked like a tornado had just run through it. The girls' backpacks, shoes, books, phones, and dirty dishes were all over the place. They knew that Crystal didn't play with them when it came to keeping a clean house. They were to clean up everything that needed to be done as soon as they got home from school. She couldn't believe that Lesley had demanded six hundred dollars for her senior trip but couldn't even do her part around the house.

"Lesley and Aisha get in here, and I mean right now!"

Both girls entered the living room wearing looks of confusion.

"Momma, what's wrong?" Aisha asked with pure concern.

"Yeah Momma, what's all the yelling for?" Lesley asked with much more attitude.

As much as Crystal loved her children, Lesley was truly a thorn in her side. Lesley acted as if she was the parent and Crystal was getting on her nerves. Since Lesley had been a small child, she'd walked around with a sense of entitlement. She never really cared about anything or anyone other than herself. Crystal still couldn't believe how close Aisha and Lesley were. Lesley had always been a great big sister and overly protective of Aisha. It was one of the few good personality traits that Lesley had.

"I'm yelling because my house is a mess. My house is to be cleaned as soon as you get home from school. You're teenagers, not little kids. Why do I have to keep repeating myself?"

"I'm sorry, Momma. I was tired, so I laid down and took a nap. I didn't mean to sleep that long. I'll clean up right now."

Crystal wasn't surprised at all at Aisha's response. She honestly was a great kid. She did what she was supposed to do most of the time and seldom gave Crystal any lip. Aisha had a way of calming Crystal down with very little effort.

"I had company, and I didn't want to be rude by cleaning up."

"Lesley, who did you have, in my house?"

"Darius."

"Wait a minute. You mean to tell me that on top of having company in my house without my permission, you had your no-good boyfriend in here?"

"What's the big deal? You have your no-good boyfriend over all the time. Who, I might add only comes around when he wants something."

Lesley stood directly in front of Crystal with her arms folded, wearing a scowl on her face, almost daring Crystal to bust a move. Crystal had learned a long time ago, that when it came to Lesley, arguing wouldn't get them anywhere. Although she was burning with anger, Crystal tried a more civil approach with her.

"Why did you have Darius in my house?"

"It's not like I invited him. He came on his own. I didn't want to be rude, so I let him in."

"What were y'all doing?"

"Momma, it's not that serious! We were just talking."

"You could have talked to him at school. When you put yourself in those predicaments you open the door to temptation. I don't want you to end up a teen parent, or worse get an incurable STD. I make rules to protect you, not punish you. This will be my last time saying this. Don't bring anyone in this house without my permission. Is that understood?"

Lesley only glared at Crystal.

"Lesley, I asked you a question. Am I understood?"

"Yes, I understand. I understand that you're a hypocrite. You do the same thing I'm doing, except it's with a married man and you think you can tell me how to run my life? And who said anything about getting pregnant? Don't worry though… if I did get pregnant I vow to be a way better mother than you. I would never put a man before my kids."

Crystal had tried being civil, but there was no reasoning with her child. Crystal pulled herself off of the couch and made her way towards Lesley. There was a defiance about Lesley that Crystal had never seen before.

"Since you're so grown, it's best that you get out of my house."

"Momma, no. Please!"

Aisha had been so quiet, that Crystal had forgotten that she was in the room.

"It's okay, Aisha. I'll gladly get out." Grabbing her backpack and cell phone, Lesley headed toward the door, which opened just as she reached for the doorknob.

"Hello, everybody," Yolanda sang.

So much had happened so quickly that Crystal had forgotten that Yolanda was coming over to visit.

"Excuse me, Aunt Yolanda. I would stay, but your friend just put me out. You may want to leave too, before you're next."

"Lesley, I'm not going to say it again," Crystal yelled.

"Well, I've never been greeted like that, before, I guess there's a first time for everything. How are you ladies doing?"

Crystal hated that her friend had to walk into a war zone, but Yolanda was no stranger to her family's shenanigans. Thankfully, Yolanda wasn't a judgmental person; she only wanted to be part of the solution. Yolanda was truly an every woman. She was beautiful, had a great body, loved the Lord, and was just an all-around good person. Her smooth caramel skin and jet-black-shoulder length dreads were always an attention getter. She had her own style, and it complimented her curvy frame. She knew who she was, whether she was wearing jeans and a t-shirt or an evening gown. There just weren't a lot of women who carried that kind of confidence. Sadly enough, Crystal had to admit she didn't carry that confidence either. That was one of the reasons Crystal kept Yolanda so close. Yolanda gave Crystal strength and courage when she needed it.

"Hey, Aunt Yolanda," Aisha came to greet Yolanda with a hug. She tried to wipe the tears before Yolanda had seen them, but it was too late. Yolanda had already seen them.

"You wipe those tears. Everything is going to be okay. Let me talk to your mom for a minute, and I'll come and talk to you later, okay?"

"Yes, ma'am." Aisha released herself from her aunt's embrace and went to her room.

Crystal was at a loss for words. She'd never thought she would see the day when she had to put her child out of the house. What frightened her most was that the older Lesley became it seemed as if their relationship mirrored her own relationship with her mom.

31

She'd always promised herself that her relationship with her girls would be way better than her relationship had been with Essie.

"Rough day, huh?" Yolanda came and sat next to Crystal and squeezed her hand.

"Honestly, it didn't get rough until I came home. I don't know what has gotten into Lesley. The last year has been down-right unbearable. It's like she fights me on everything."

"You don't want to hear this, but you're what has gotten into her."

"Excuse me."

"When did Lesley start to act out?" Yolanda asked.

"It seems like an eternity. I don't know. Maybe a couple years ago."

"Which is right around the time you and Marcus started to get serious."

"What are you trying to say?" Crystal rose off the couch, nothing short of irritated, and the smirk on Yolanda's face didn't help the cause.

"What's so funny?"

"You get so defensive about everything. Calm down and let me explain what I mean."

Easing back onto the couch, Crystal sat with her body stiffened. She wouldn't even look directly at Yolanda; she gave her the side eye instead.

"Crystal, ever since you started seeing Marcus, he has become your priority. It's like your world doesn't turn if he's not a part of it. I think your girls, especially Lesley, are feeling neglected."

"I think you're trying to say I don't love my kids, and I resent that."

"That's not what I'm saying at all. I just think right now your children aren't your number one priority."

"Yolanda, I would die for my children. I would do everything in my power to protect them. I don't know why Lesley can't see that."

"Did you ever think that Lesley is trying to protect you as well? Nobody wants to see their mother hurt and used. When you hurt, your children hurt as well. When they see that you keep allowing the pain, their pain turns into anger."

"I never looked at it like that, but Marcus is a good man. Why am I the only person who can see that?"

"Let me say this first, Crystal. My number one concern is you and my nieces. Marcus is a non-factor to me. You don't want to hear the truth, but I wouldn't be your friend if I didn't tell you. There is no 'relationship' with you and Marcus. He's married. The only relationship that's legit is the one between him and his wife. And you're not his only mistress. He sleeps around with other women from the church. The rumor is he got some woman pregnant up there and, now he's trying to cover it up."

"I know."

"What do you mean, you know?"

Crystal was so embarrassed to admit that she'd basically given Marcus a pass to sleep with any woman that he wanted when she had given him the money for the abortion.

"I gave him the money to cover up the pregnancy, so his wife wouldn't find out."

Yolanda look bewildered, and Crystal knew what she was thinking without her saying a word.

"I don't want to hear it Yolanda. You wouldn't understand. I love that man."

"But, does he love you back? That is the question? Your relationship with him is conditional, and it's ruining your relationship with Lesley."

"What do you know about a relationship? It's been years since you been on a date. Ms. Independent. That's what you call yourself, right?

For a brief second the jig towards Yolanda felt good, but the feeling didn't last long. Yolanda's expression went from concern to pain. As beautiful as Yolanda was, dating had never been her strong suit. Yolanda would never admit it, but Crystal was sure that Yolanda had given up on dating all together.

"Let's just change the subject." Yolanda said.

"I agree."

That was just like Yolanda to be the bigger person. Crystal couldn't be happier that Yolanda had decided to drop the subject. She loved her friend and didn't want to argue with her.

"Well, Aisha is good as always, and as you just saw Lesley is no longer a resident of this house. And something is telling me that she's having sex."

"I'm sorry to hear that. Ask God for guidance in raising your girls. He won't steer you wrong."

"I know you're right. Look at my house, it's a mess. I can't believe these girls didn't clean up. Let me get up off this couch and clean up and cook Aisha some dinner."

Crystal tried to rise, but Yolanda used her hand to block her.

"You lay here and get some rest. I'll do it."

"Yolanda, you don't have to do that."

"I know I don't, but you really need to relax"

"Okay, while you're cleaning up, let me tell you about the conversation that I overheard at work."

Yolanda set the dirty dishes she'd just picked up back down on the coffee table and plopped back onto the couch. "Don't hold back. Spill the tea, girl."

"Yolanda, you're a mess. I thought you were about to clean up? Anyway, why did First Lady Davis accuse Pastor Davis of having an affair with me? I guess it's trouble on the home front. First Lady ain't no fool, she knows there are women who would love to stick their hooks in her man. "

"I hate to ask you this, but is it true?"

"Yolanda!"

"I'm sorry, but Marcus is married, and that didn't stop you from seeing him."

Crystal's ears grew warm with embarrassment, but because of her current arrangement with Marcus, she had to admit it was a legitimate question. She couldn't help but wonder if she was behaving like some Jezebel? She decided against the thought because she was only sleeping with one man.

"No, I'm not having an affair with him. I will say this, though, if she keeps accusing us, I'm going to bring her accusations to life."

"Really," Yolanda said.

Crystal could hear the disgust in Yolanda's voice.

"No girl, I'm only joking...well, maybe I'm not," Crystal said with a purr.

"You know what Crystal? You're the bad girl everyone wants to be but is too afraid to let it show."

"I know. That's why you keep me around.

"Girl, hush. I'm going to finish cleaning, so I can start cooking.

Chapter 5

Crystal tried everything within her power to stay focused on work. The church's annual blood drive was this coming Sunday, and it was her responsibility to make sure everything was ready. If she didn't get her head in the game quick, the blood drive would be a disaster. It had been over a month since Crystal had heard from Marcus, and her pride had taken a hit. Once again she'd been victimized by broken promises and sex-capades. Her aching heart couldn't understand why Marcus would do this to her. She'd loved him to the depths of her soul, and she wasn't ready to walk away from the best man she'd ever loved.

She'd lied and told Pastor Davis she wasn't feeling well last Sunday, hoping to catch Marcus preaching in the pulpit. To her surprise, Marcus hadn't been at church himself. Strangely enough, she was positive that she kept feeling his wife staring at her. Did Mrs. Powers know who she was? She'd always done her best to be as discreet as possible. Crystal snuck out in the middle of service and told herself not to visit Freewill again.

"Crystal, I need the parking lot to be emptied by three today so I can pressure wash the concrete."

Crystal looked up to see her buddy Rodney. He was the church maintenance man for New Hope and loved by every employee that worked there. He had the kind of personality that fit everywhere. Crystal often teased him with the nickname Chameleon because he had a way of making everyone feel so comfortable when he was around.

"Hey, Rodney. I already made the announcement so everyone would know. I'm going to remind everyone at two–thirty, just to make sure."

"That will work," said Rodney as he pulled a chair up to Crystal's desk.

She wasn't really in the mood to socialize, but she did need to be distracted from her thoughts.

"Are you participating in the blood drive this year?" Crystal asked.

"You know I hate needles. After being poked and stuck so many times as a child, I vowed to stay as far away from them as possible."

Crystal recalled Rodney telling her that he was born with a rare disease that had caused him to go into kidney failure at a young age. By the time he was ten, he had no kidney function at all and had been forced to be on dialysis. When Rodney turned seventeen, he experienced what doctors called a medical miracle, for people of faith, knew it was all God, and his kidneys had begun to function on their own at one hundred percent.

"I'm surprised at you, Rodney. God basically gave you a second chance at life, and you never take advantage of the opportunity to give life back. What's up with that?"

"Just call it a phobia of mine."

"Tell me what I have to do to get that needle in your arm on Sunday?"

Rodney leaned back in his chair and a smirk crept on his face. He had the deepest dimple on his left cheek whenever he smiled, which was always appealing to the ladies.

"Let me take you to dinner. And don't give me that junk about messing with our work chemistry."

Crystal had walked herself right into that one. She internally scolded herself.

"How about I think about it and get back to you later in the week?"

Rodney sat up straight in his chair, giving Crystal direct eye contact.

"While you're considering my proposition, I'll be considering yours. I'll touch base with you later."

Crystal watched as Rodney left her office. She'd known he had a crush on her and he was surely handsome enough. The thing was that Crystal had wanted more for herself than settling down with a maintenance man. She was no ordinary woman, and no ordinary man would do for her. She knew most people would call her shallow for thinking in such a way, but what else could she say? She wanted what she wanted.

Chapter 6

Crystal parked her car and surveyed the landscape around her. She tried her best to hide her car in the over-grown grass in the big country field. How Marcus had found this place, Crystal would never know. She'd lived in Dallas her entire life and had never known this rural part of the city. She couldn't even believe that she'd made the eighty-mile journey to come, but another day had passed and still no Marcus. Her heart refused to continue to suffer the heartache she'd been experiencing over the past month. Before she knew it, she had lied to Pastor Davis, saying there had been an emergency with her daughter and she needed to leave right away. Her broken heart had Crystal acting out of character. Lying to her boss wasn't something she wanted to continue, but at the moment she was desperate.

She and Marcus had a secret getaway that he'd purchased just for them. He often told her he would come to this place because it allowed him to meditate and talk with God without the distractions of the city. She was pretty sure God didn't look kindly on Marcus committing adultery, though.

He'd promised Crystal that once they were married they could add more on to the home. Marcus had made Crystal promise that she would never come to the house on her own. The request didn't make sense to her, but again, she wanted to make him happy, so she willingly obliged. She hated going against his wishes, but he'd left her no choice.

As she made her way closer to the house, she was able to see his car in the distance. She felt a surge of relief because she would finally get to see her baby. She couldn't believe that she was so excited to see him after the way he'd been ignoring her.

Before she knew it, her pace had begun to quicken until she was running full speed to the house, but the image she saw through the window nearly took her breath away. There was Marcus caressing another woman's body in the same way he once touched hers. Their naked bodies were intertwined and the mystery woman had thrown her head back in full ecstasy. The same ecstasy she had once experienced.

Crystal could taste the bile rising in her throat. The longer she watched, the more nauseated she became. Before she knew it, her lunch covered the window ledge. It hurt like hell to watch, but she couldn't turn away. Even through tear-filled eyes, she could see everything so vividly. Forcing her feet to move, Crystal backed away from the house slowly and headed towards her car.

———

Crystal stared straight ahead as she hugged the curves of the winding road. "How could I be so stupid?" she asked herself. So many emotions ran through her, but hurt and embarrassment were the most dominant. She'd had her fair share of disappointments with men, but never had she experienced a pain like this. Crystal now knew what real heartache felt like. Marcus was the man of her dreams; the man who was going to make her a first lady. And now she was back to nothing.

"I give you two years, Marcus, and you can't even tell me it's over? This is the last time I will be hurt by a man. This is last time I will be hurt by a man!" she yelled at the top of her lungs. She knew she must have looked like a mad woman as the tears flowed uncontrollably and snot dripped from her nose into her mouth, but none of that mattered. She had to face the fact that their relationship was over, but she would accept that conclusion once she made it home. The remaining drive home would allow her time to cry her heart out and sulk in her pain.

Chapter 7

Crystal stared out of her bedroom window, deep in thought. The ceiling fan circulated a cool breeze throughout the room. The cool air caressing her face helped ease some of her tension. It had been the first time she had relaxed since seeing Marcus with another woman. With the blood drive, she hadn't had time to focus on the pain.

The blood drive had been successful, as it was every year. This year, she had solicited the most donors since the blood drive began. She'd had even convinced Rodney to donate as well. She did have to promise him a date in return. She hated to admit that she'd only accepted the invitation because she was on a rebound. She always got over a bad break up by dating someone new. Yolanda always told her that a Band-Aid wouldn't fix a gunshot wound. Her advice may have been true, but it was too painful to just let the healing process happen. It was so much easier playing it safe.

Realizing she didn't feel the air on her face anymore, Crystal looked up at the fan. The fan blades went from spinning to a crawl.

She prayed that the fan was only broken. She reached for her remote on her nightstand and pressed the ON button on the remote so hard she got a cramp in her finger. No matter how hard she pressed, the TV wouldn't turn on. At this point, Crystal knew exactly what was happening, but she didn't want to admit it to herself. She reached for the lamp that sat on her nightstand next to her plush, king-sized bed. Crystal made several attempts at turning the knob, but the lamp refused to turn on.

Her electricity had been turned off, and she had no idea where she was going to get the money. She knew she had to figure something out soon. Pastor Davis would be over shortly to pick the report up that he needed for a meeting. Crystal had mistaken the file for something else and brought it home by accident. How embarrassing would it be for her boss to come to her home with no electricity? What would he think of her?

Then there was Aisha; she didn't want Aisha to go through this again. Three times in one year was enough to last a lifetime. Aisha had never voiced her frustration, but who wouldn't be frustrated to come home to no electricity countless times? She cursed herself for giving Marcus the money for the abortion.

She would have to call her mother. The problem wouldn't be getting the money from Essie, but what she would have to endure to get it. She didn't have any other options. Hopefully, she could get her mother to pay the bill before Pastor Davis arrived. Knowing she couldn't prolong the call any longer, Crystal reached for her iPhone. She found her mother's name in her contacts and pressed the call button. Crystal listened to the ringer until she heard her mother's voice.

"Hello." Her mother's voice was groggy. Crystal looked at the time on her phone; it was almost nine-thirty. She had forgotten that her mother was a night owl and didn't get out of bed before ten, and that was on a good day.

"Momma, it's Crystal. I really need a favor." Crystal braced herself for the avalanche of words that were about to come.

"Crystal, what do you need now? I just gave you five hundred dollars last month."

Crystal picked her next words carefully. She needed her mother, and didn't want to say anything that would put her on the defensive.

"My electricity just got cut off. Will you please loan me the money until I get paid next week? I don't want to put my girls through this again."

"Stop with all the antics. Why is it that you never consider your girls until the aftermath has already happened? One of your girls isn't even at home with you; she's here with me. You do remember putting her out, don't you?"

Lying back on her pillow and closing her eyes, she hoped that her mother's tirade would be over soon enough. She really needed to get her electricity back on before Pastor Davis arrived.

"Momma, are you going to let me borrow the money or not? I really need to get the electricity back on before Pastor Davis gets here."

"Did you say Pastor Davis is coming over?"

Crystal could have sworn she heard a hint of a purr in her mother's voice when she said Pastor Davis's name. She knew her mother was attracted to him, but she prayed her mother wasn't about to start any funny business with her boss. She didn't need any more drama in her life.

"Yes, he's coming. For work."

"I'll be over in the next thirty minutes."

"Why? You can use your credit card and pay over the phone. We've done this before."

"I'll pay the bill as soon as I get there. See you in a few."

―――

"You know, Crystal, despite how irresponsible you've been, you have somehow managed to take great care of your grand-mother's antique mirror." Crystal watched as Essie touched up her make up in the mirror for the third time. Her mother had waltzed in wearing her Sunday's best, which only meant that Essie had come to put on a show.

"You know how much that mirror means to me. Every time I see it I think about Grandmother. It's the only thing that I have left of hers, and stop fixing your makeup. You do realize Pastor Davis is a happily married man?" Crystal couldn't hide her frustration over her mother's presence. She really did try to be cordial with her, but Essie always gave her reason to be nasty.

"This is coming from the same woman who has been waiting on a certain married man to leave his wife? And it's not nice to be rude to someone that just gave you three hundred dollars to get your electricity turned back on."

Crystal looked up and saw Essie staring at her through the mirror. Essie's eyes dared Crystal to challenge her, but Crystal knew better. Whether Crystal wanted to admit it or not, Essie had come through for her once again. She didn't know how she would have explained herself to Pastor Davis if he had come when her electricity was shut off. Diverting her eyes to the TV, Crystal decided to play nice with her mother. She knew all too well if she stepped on Essie's toes, she was sure to make her pay for it.

"I really appreciate you giving me the money to get my lights back on?"

"No dear, I didn't give you the money...I loaned it to you. Make no mistake; I want every penny back that you owe me. You may want to think twice the next time you decide to give your money away to a no-good dog."

Crystal ignored the last statement; she really wasn't trying to start an argument. She didn't want Pastor Davis walking into a warzone.

"Essie, I can't believe you're making me pay you back. You're not hard up for money; you just want something to hold over my head."

Essie stopped looking at herself in the mirror and marched up to Crystal. "Yes, you're going to pay me back. Your bills aren't my respons..."

Knock. Knock. Knock.

"That must be Pastor Davis. Momma, I want you to be on your best behavior."

"You don't have to worry... Pastor Davis is definitely going to get the best of me."

"Momma!"

"Who is it?"

"Pastor Davis."

Crystal gave herself a once over in the mirror. She caught Essie staring at her out of the corner of her eye.

"Who are you trying to look good for? I certainly hope not for the married Pastor Davis?"

"Momma, please." Opening the door, Crystal stood hypnotized by what stood before her. She had always thought Pastor Davis was a very handsome man, but today he reminded her of something so beautiful that he could have been on view at a museum. Pastor Davis always kept himself well groomed, but today his appearance was impeccable. The tailor-made suit that wrapped his body was only an added incentive.

"Are you okay, Crystal? You look as if I startled you."

Crystal couldn't find any words. Actually, she was afraid that if she opened her mouth something inappropriate would escape. She had already created an awkward situation at the office the other day; she certainly didn't want to put her foot in her mouth again.

"Pastor Davis, please excuse my thoughtless daughter; I really don't know what has gotten into her. Well…I do, but that's not important," Essie said as she sashayed her way toward Pastor Davis.

Essie's words snapped Crystal out of her daze. She had to get Essie out of her house now, before she embarrassed everybody in the room.

"Pastor Davis, please excuse my rudeness. You did catch me off guard. You remember my mother, Essie, don't you?"

"Of course he remembers me. I've been known to make quite an impression." Essie raised her hand for Pastor Davis to kiss it.

Crystal had to stifle her laugh when Pastor Davis took her hand and shook it instead of giving the kiss Essie longed for.

Crystal grabbed the file from the coffee table and handed it to Pastor Davis. "I'm pretty sure you have a busy schedule ahead of you. Here's the file you needed."

"I actually do need to get out of here, but I needed to speak with you about something before I go."

"Okay, let me walk Momma out, and I'll be right with you." Crystal didn't give Essie any time to protest. She grabbed her purse from the couch and escorted Essie towards the door.

"Crystal, what are you…"

"I refuse to let you embarrass me in front of the Pastor," Crystal whispered into Essie's ear. "All right, Momma. I'll be in touch," Crystal said as she practically pushed Essie out the door.

"What did you need to talk to me about?"

"I'm having a business meeting with a few colleagues next week, and I need you to attend. You have such great understanding of the reports and the data behind them. I was hoping you could assist me with this?

Crystal's heart skipped a beat. She couldn't help but wonder if this was just a business dinner or more.

"That's no problem, Pastor. I'll be more than happy to attend."

"Thanks, Crystal. I'll leave you to enjoy the rest of your day, and I'll see you tomorrow.

"You too, Pastor." Crystal followed Pastor Davis to the door and couldn't help but think that things were beginning to look up for her.

Chapter 8

Crystal sat in the employee's break room at the church. Being that she was broke until payday, which was still a week away, she was forced to bring her lunch to work. Crystal preferred to get out the office for lunch, but with no extra money to spare, she couldn't afford to have a preference. At one point in time, she and Marcus would sneak away for lunch. Sometimes they would go and eat at a restaurant, and other times they would indulge in each other. Those were some of her sweetest memories. Swallowing hard to fight back the tears, Crystal focused on the *Essence* magazine in front of her.

An article caught her eye as she turned the page from a L'Oreal makeup advertisement. "Ten Signs that You're Dating Mr. Wrong." She could have used this article two years ago. Sign number one read: He Just Won't Commit. She couldn't read anymore because she wasn't ready to admit that the man she loved had played her. Her heart knew the truth, but her pride wasn't ready to accept defeat.

"Crystal, your mom is here. You could have warned a brother that she was so fine. If that's what you're going to look like in the next twenty years...baby I'm all yours."

Crystal tried to control her laughter, but she never could with Rodney.

"Boy you're crazy, and stop looking at my momma." Crystal said as she playfully slapped Rodney on the back of the head.

"I'm just saying you could have given a brother a heads up."

As Crystal approached Essie in the back foyer, she laughed to herself. Her mother was still turning heads at her age. Giving her the once over, Crystal had to admit that Essie did look good. The fitted, knee length leopard print dress with the hot-pink stilettos were a dangerous combination, and Essie wore them well. Her hair was pulled up in a bun and her tastefully applied makeup was an added incentive. Essie had just turned fifty-four and could still pass for her early forties. She had always taken great care of herself, and she worked out regularly.

Crystal assumed that she had gotten her good looks from her mother. Her father had walked out on Essie the very minute he got wind that she was pregnant. Crystal tried to pretend that not knowing her father didn't bother her, but the little girl inside of her cried out quite often for the father she never got to meet. In Crystal's eyes, one of the worst feelings in the world was not being wanted by one of the very people who created you.

"Essie, I hope this is an emergency. You know I don't like folks bothering me while I'm at work. I think it's so unprofessional."

"Crystal, please. I have something very important to discuss with you about Aisha."

"Is she all right?"

"Yeah…well, if you consider the circumstances."

"What circumstance? Will you please come out with it? I don't have time; I need to get back to work."

"Fine. Aisha is pregnant, and she's determined to keep this baby."

"Aisha, pregnant? My Aisha…that can't be."

"She thinks she's about four months along. She's not for sure… she hasn't been to the doctor yet."

Before she knew it, Crystal was hunched over the trash, heaving until she had thrown up her entire lunch. When she could gather herself enough to look up, Essie held out some tissue and a bottle of water to her.

"I figured this would happen. You always carried your nerves in your stomach. Are you okay?"

Crystal took the tissue and wiped her mouth. She was too afraid to drink the water; she didn't think her stomach could handle it right now. Just the thought of Aisha being pregnant made her stomach queasy, and she surely didn't want to consider the thought of being a grandmother at the age of thirty-seven. Aisha saw how hard the struggle was for them when she was growing up. Why would she do such a thing?

"How did I miss this? She keeps her head so deep in books, I didn't even know she was interested in boys."

"How could you see it? Your head is so deep in Marcus's behind."

"That's not true."

"It is true. Anyway, you need to get Aisha to the doctor ASAP."

"She's not keeping the baby."

Crystal knew Essie wasn't going to let it end so easily. The incredulous look Essie wore confirmed what Crystal already knew.

"Crystal, we need to help Aisha be the best mother possible. Forcing her to have an abortion will destroy her."

"Who is going to financially care for this baby? Aisha doesn't have a job, and I can't afford to provide for a baby."

"Yet, you can provide for a married man. Interesting."

At this point Crystal was seething. She didn't want to continue this discussion at her job. The angrier she became, the louder she got. She hadn't realized they'd attracted a small audience. Her chaos had even brought Pastor Davis out of his office.

"Essie, you need to leave. I can't deal with this right now."

"That's the problem. You never want to deal with anything pertaining to your kids, but let Marcus call with any kind of issue and you're going to make it your business to help him. When are your children going to become a priority to you?"

"I have to get back to work; I've listened to your foolishness long enough."

Chapter 9

Crystal couldn't believe a week had already passed since Pastor Davis asked her to accompany him to his business meeting. So much had transpired in that week. Finding out Aisha was pregnant had definitely been the highlight, and not in a good way. After Essie had dropped that bomb, Crystal thought she would have a nervous breakdown. She honestly didn't feel she could have taken one more thing happening to her. Happy that she had something positive to distract her from her chaotic life, Crystal admired herself in the full-length mirror in her bedroom. She looked good, and nobody would be able to tell her otherwise. Crystal was positive that even the faithful Pastor Davis would have to do a double take after he saw her tonight. The coral sheath dress that she wore with the matching jacket gave her a sexy but classy look. She made sure the dress accented all of her curves, but didn't cling to them. Crystal completed the outfit with a simple black pump and the gold-cross necklace Marcus had given her for her birthday last year.

Seeing the necklace made Crystal realize that she hadn't thought about him all day. Lifting her head and closing her eyes Crystal gave

God a silent praise of thanks. She'd never thought she would be able to go a minute without thinking about him, let alone a day.

"Hey, Momma," Aisha said as she poked her head through the cracked door.

"Hey. You can come in." Crystal knew that she couldn't avoid her daughter any longer. Crystal watched as Aisha climbed into her bed. Her volleyball-sized belly was very visible now. Crystal couldn't help but wonder if Aisha had hid her belly that well or if she had been so distracted that she'd missed it all together. Her baby was having a baby, and Crystal didn't know how to handle the situation.

"You look beautiful, Momma. Where are you going?"

"I'm escorting Pastor Davis to a business dinner."

She looked at Aisha through the mirror and caught the sadness in her eyes. Crystal knew that Aisha hadn't liked what she had just heard, but Aisha kept it to herself out of fear of being disrespectful.

"What's on your mind, Aisha?"

"Shouldn't First Lady Davis be going to the business dinner with Pastor Davis?"

Crystal already didn't like where this conversation was going, but she'd opened Pandora's box and there was no turning back now.

"His wife couldn't make it, and that's why I'm going with him. Something tells me this is a loaded question. What's up, Aisha?"

"It just seems like you only see men that already have wives and everybody knows about it, and it's like you don't care."

"What I care about is you being a teenage mom. How could you do this, Aisha? You see our struggle. You put this family in a really bad predicament."

"I'm sorry, Momma. I never wanted to disappoint you. It just happened, and now I can't take it back. Please don't hate me."

Almost as a reflex Aisha grabbed a pillow and covered her belly.

Crystal remembered feeling the same way when she was pregnant with Lesley. That had to be the darkest time in her life. No matter how angry and disappointed she was with Aisha, her empathy was greater.

"Never could I hate you. You're my child, and I'll always love you. Let's finish this conversation later. I need to finish getting ready."

"Momma, can I ask you one more question before you go?"

"Sure."

"Are you going to let Lesley come home anytime soon?"

Crystal knew it would only be a matter of time before Aisha would start asking about her sister. The two had an inseparable bond between them. Lesley may not have been the best daughter, but she was an awesome big sister. It had been that way since the day Crystal brought Aisha home. Crystal was actually surprised it had taken Aisha this long to ask about Lesley.

"Why do you think I should let her come home? You saw how your sister disrespected me in my house."

"I messed up too, Ma. Why do I get your grace and she doesn't?"

"We'll talk later, Aisha."

Knock. Knock. Knock.

"That's Pastor Davis. Go let him in while I finish my makeup."

"Yes, ma'am."

———

On the ride to the restaurant, Crystal did more listening than talking, which had always been a struggle for her. Pastor Davis really had a great sense of humor. She'd always know it was there, but she guessed he relaxed more outside of the church. The more she listened, the more it confirmed that Pastor Davis was the type of man she could see herself with. Not wanting to fall into the same webs of deceit that she had created with Marcus, she promised herself that she wouldn't fall head first for Pastor Davis. If Pastor Davis wanted any type of relationship, he would have to earn her love instead of her just giving it away. Her foolish days were long gone.

"Crystal, we're here. Do you have all the reports we need?"

"Yes. I have everything you need." Crystal wondered if Pastor Davis had caught the hint. Crystal slipped the files into her bag and waited for the valet to help her out of the black Cadillac Escalade. She knew she could get used to this lifestyle. Never had Marcus taken her to a place that was so exquisite. She hadn't seen it before, but breaking up with Marcus had been the best thing that could have ever happened to her. She had settled for chicken, when there was a juicy steak dangling right in front of her.

As they approached their table, Crystal could see two men at the table chatting. Pastor Davis hadn't explained who they were, so she had no idea how to greet them. She assumed Pastor Davis would handle all of this.

"Gentlemen, it's a pleasure to see you." Pastor Davis extended his hand to each of them as they rose from their seat. "This is Crystal. She'll be helping me breakdown the numbers to each of you."

Both men extended their hand to Crystal. Pastor Davis pulled out Crystal's seat while introducing the men as Bishop Dane Jackson and Pastor Robert McCullum.

"It's a pleasure to meet each of you," Crystal said.

"You're sure a sight for sore eyes. Pastor Davis, your wife is simply stunning," said Pastor McCullum as he took his seat.

Crystal waited for Pastor Davis to correct Pastor McCullum about the wife comment, but when he didn't, Crystal just rolled with it.

"Thank you," Pastor Davis said while squeezing Crystal's hand.

"We took the liberty of having the waiter bring out water and the menus while we waited," said Bishop Jackson.

"We appreciate that," Pastor Davis said.

The entire experience gave Crystal goosebumps. She'd always imagined this life for herself, and she couldn't wait to be a first lady. She knew firsthand how to run a church, so being Pastor Davis's wife and right hand would be an asset for him. Crystal took it all in as the men discussed the project for the new youth center for disadvantaged kids. Everyone was on the same page and believed the youth center would really benefit the community. Now, it was Crystal's turn to break down the project cost and seal the deal.

"Crystal, are you ready?" Pastor Davis asked as he adjusted his tie.

"Yes. Gentlemen the folders that I'm passing out to you have the breakdown of the cost to build the youth center and the projection of the cost to keep it running for the next five years."

Crystal waited for the men's reactions as they turned from page to page reviewing the reports. Crystal knew she had out done herself on this one. She'd researched this project for weeks to make sure she had everything covered. Pastor Davis had been so excited about the project, and she didn't want to disappoint him.

"Crystal, you've done an impeccable job," Bishop Jackson praised.

"I have to concur. Everything looks good. All we need now is to get everything finalized with our lawyers so we can proceed," said Pastor McCullum.

"Thank you," was all Crystal could muster. She was sure she was cheesing like a Cheshire cat. She really hoped this would make Pastor Davis see her in another light. Unlike his wife, she could assist with his day-to-day activities as well as his big projects. They would be an unstoppable force, the Gospel's version of Bonnie and Clyde.

———

Crystal was in full relaxation mode. Pastor's Escalade rode so smooth and the jazz flowing through the speakers was an added touch.

"I want to apologize about you being put on the spot about being my wife."

Crystal had hoped he would bring that up. She was curious to know why Pastor Davis didn't clear up the misunderstanding.

"No problem. Mistakes happen."

"I was worried that if I would have corrected them a red flag would have gone up."

"What do you mean, a red flag?"

"If I would have told them that my wife and I are having marital problems and that she refuses to support me, they might have thought I wouldn't be capable of running a youth center."

Crystal wasn't following Pastor Davis, so she sat up in her seat as if doing so would give her a clearer understanding of what he was saying. "I'm sorry, Pastor. I still don't follow."

"Basically, I didn't want to give them the impression that my home wasn't in order. As a man, I should always have my house in order. "

Crystal honestly didn't know how to respond to Pastor Davis words, so she didn't. Instead, she settled back into the leather seat and let the jazz ease her mind for the remainder of the ride.

Chapter 10

Crystal eyed the door of the restaurant, hoping she would see Yolanda when she came in. It was their monthly girl's day, a tradition they had started about ten years ago. Once a month they would have an outing where they could relax from the stress of life. On this day, they had to leave their problems at home and just have fun. They alternated who chose the place and who paid for it. This month was Yolanda's turn, and Crystal couldn't be more grateful. She was still trying to play catch up from the last couple of month's unexpected expenses.

By the looks of the restaurant, this place wouldn't have been in Crystal's price range anyway. Yolanda had chosen the Grand Lux, located next to the Galleria Mall in North Dallas. The Grand Lux's décor carried a feel of elegance. The marble floors and intricate ceiling and wall decorations put Crystal in the mind of a European café. Yolanda had a great job, wasn't married and didn't have any children. She could afford to live the good life and splurge on herself.

Buzz. Buzz. Buzz.

Crystal looked down at her phone and saw Marcus's name flash on the screen. That was the fourth time he'd called her in the last hour. He had his nerve to call her back to back, expecting her to answer. After, seeing him with another woman in his arms, there was nothing left for them to talk about. Crystal never thought she would ever be over Marcus, but the time had come, and she welcomed it.

Crystal's phone vibrated once again, alerting her that she had a text message. She had to laugh to herself when she read the words.

Baby, I know you're mad because I've been so distant. There's so much going on in my life, but I really need you, so please call me.

The only thing Marcus needed Crystal for was money. She refused to continue to supply that need for him. Crystal deleted the text without a second thought.

"What is so interesting in your phone? I've just been standing here and not once did you look up?"

Crystal answered her friend with a smile and rose from the table to give her a hug. Yolanda looked good, but she always did. The sophisticated street style really worked for her. The BCBG clutch she carried was an added plus. "Nothing, just ignoring Marcus."

"You... ignoring Marcus? He must have really messed up this time," Yolanda said as she took her seat.

"He really did, and I'm so done with him. I don't want to talk about Marcus, so let's change the subject."

"That's the best news that I've heard in a long time. I'm very proud of you...I know it wasn't an easy decision."

Crystal took a sip of her ice water and carefully thought how she was going to say her next words. The cold water felt good sliding down her throat. Yolanda was her best friend, and she didn't keep anything from her. But Crystal knew what she was about to tell Yolanda wouldn't go over well.

"Actually, Yolanda, the decision wasn't very hard at all. I think I'm seeing someone else and he's made the transition very easy."

"Hello, ladies. I hope you're doing well today. My name is Mindy and I'll be your waitress. Would you like to start out with anything to drink or an appetizer?"

"I'll have vodka and tonic. Matter of fact, make it a double," Yolanda said.

Crystal glanced at her Michael Kors watch and then eyed Yolanda as she completed her order.

"I'll just have a glass of your Pinot," she said. Handing the drink menu back to the waitress.

"Okay, ladies, I'll have those drinks right out to you. Do you need a few minutes to order?"

Crystal answered the waitress with a nod.

"Okay, I'll be right back."

As soon as the waitress was out of earshot, Crystal began questioning her friend. "A vodka and tonic at lunch time…I'm sorry, a double vodka. What's going on?"

"Nothing. I just need to relax. It's been a long a week."

"Yolanda, you've always been a horrible liar. What's up?" Crystal knew it had to be something heavy, because Yolanda wouldn't even give her eye contact.

"I'm just preparing myself for your news."

"What's that supposed to mean?"

"Who's your new man?"

"Pastor Davis."

"Why do you keep doing this to yourself? Don't you think you deserve more?"

"Yolanda, I know you're worried about me, and I love you for that. But I need you to trust me when I say I won't ever let a man make a fool out of me again. Marcus was the last time. I got this."

Crystal's phone started buzzing again. Looking down at her phone, she didn't recognize the number. Since she'd been ignoring Marcus's calls, she wouldn't be surprised if he'd tried to call her from another number. She had some choice words for Marcus, and the Grand Lux wouldn't be the proper place to deliver them.

"Are you going to get that?"

"No. I'm pretty sure it's Marcus calling me from a different number. I don't have anything to say to him."

"You're serious about ending this thing, huh?"

"So, serious."

Crystal's phone alerted her that she had a voicemail. She knew she needed to end their relationship properly. She'd reach out to him later this evening to do just that.

Chapter 11

Crystal was finally back at home after hanging with Yolanda all day. Her cheeks still hurt from laughing so hard. That Yolanda was a handful, but Crystal was positive that Yolanda would say the same about her. Crystal hadn't had an entire day to herself in quite sometime. Aisha was spending the night with Essie and Lesley, so Crystal honestly didn't know what to do with herself. She would have loved to spend some time with Pastor Davis, but their relationship was too new and she promised herself not to force anything.

Crystal also knew that she couldn't entertain a new relationship without getting closure from the old one. After the way Marcus had been blowing her phone up she knew what she had to do. Grabbing her phone, she remembered the voicemail Marcus left earlier that day. She decided to listen to the message before giving Marcus a call.

Gabrielle Beasley

Hello Ms. Long...This is Elizabeth from Carson's Blood Center. Last week you donated at New Hope Church. If you would please return my call I would like to discuss your donation with you. Please give me a call at 817-555-7979.

Caught off guard by the message, Crystal didn't know what to think, but decided it was best to worry about it tomorrow. Right now all she could do is handle one thing at a time. She glanced at the time, it was seven-thirty, too late to call Marcus. She knew he'd probably be spending time with his family and wouldn't be able to talk. It looked like she would have to wait until tomorrow for this as well.

Crystal couldn't help but to think how her life had spiraled completely out of control. Leaning back in her mocha-colored suede recliner, which was positioned next to her window, she stared at the stars that lit up the dark blue sky. That's when she realized that she hadn't talked to God in a very long time. She had just been going and going – it made sense why her life was turned upside down. Crystal couldn't recall the last time she'd made God the center of her life or even a portion of her life. How did she work for a church under one of the most prominent pastors in Dallas, TX and fail to have God as the center of her life? Something was seriously wrong with that picture, and she was the only one who could fix it.

Grabbing her Bible off the nightstand, she prayed and asked God to speak to her heart through his Word. Opening her Bible, she fell on the book of Galatians 5: 16 -18.

*So I say live by the Spirit and you will not gratify
the desires of the sinful nature. For the sinful
nature desires what is contrary to the Spirit and
the Spirit what is contrary to the sinful nature.
They are in conflict with each other, so that you
do not do what you want. But if you are led by the
Spirit, you are not under law.*

Crystal closed her Bible and meditated on the words she finished reading. She thought about how the passage related to her own life. One thing she knew for sure was that she hadn't been walking in the spirit. Her flesh was in complete control, and she didn't even know how to contain it.

Crystal always knew that sleeping with married men, men of God at that, was definitely a sin, and she knew she would be punished for her behavior. All she wanted was a man to call her own. It wasn't her fault that only married pastors seemed to be interested in her. Come to think of it, that's all Essie had ever attracted as well. She came into this world an accident, and maybe somewhere down the line Crystal had figured that being with a man of God would help her make things right with God.

Falling on her knees for the first time in months, Crystal prayed with an open heart.

"Father, it's Crystal. I know you haven't heard from me in a while, but here I am. I'm crying out to you because I'm scared and I don't know what to do. My life is in complete shambles.

Gabrielle Beasley

I've made every wrong turn possible, and now I'm asking you to make my path straight. My longing for a man is destroying my relationships with the people that I love, and it's just plain wrong. The thing is I don't know how to make the desire go away and learn to chase after you. Yet it's you who knows my heart's earnest desires. I'm relinquishing the wheel and giving it back to you. I'm believing you're going to work my mess out for my good, and I thank you in advance, in Jesus name, Amen."

Chapter 12

One by one, Crystal watched the goose bumps pop up on her skin. She had finally gotten back with the blood center after they left the voicemail about her donation. Now, she sat inside of a cold office reading all the posters plastered on the wall: *Giving Blood Saves Lives, Give Hope Give Life, Give the Gift of Life.* She'd checked her watch for the third time and fifteen minutes had passed. Crystal never understood the purpose of making an appointment if you still had to wait. She needed to get back to work; her lunch break was almost over.

Knock. Knock. Knock.

"Hi, Mrs. Long. I'm sorry to keep you waiting. My name is Rachel Watson. I was the drive coordinator for New Hope."

"Yes, I remember speaking with you over the phone while I was planning the blood drive. I'm not trying to be rude, but I really wish you could have done this over the phone. I'm really pressed for time."

Up until that moment Crystal hadn't been the least bit worried about this appointment. But the fact that Rachel hadn't smiled once since she entered the office began to set off alarms. Yes, she was pleasant enough, but her expression said there was more to the story.

"Discussing your blood work is confidential, Ms. Long. Legally, we're only able to give your results in person."

Rachel took a seat behind the wooden desk and closed what Crystal assumed was her chart.

"I want to first let you know that when a donor gives blood, each donation goes through a series of tests for infectious diseases, such as Hepatitis B and C, Human T-Lymphotropic Virus, Syphilis, and the Human Immunodeficiency Virus know as HIV. Each test is run multiple times just to make sure there are no inconsistencies."

"Rachel, you're starting to scare me. Please tell me what's going on."

"Crystal, the HIV test shows antibody reactive."

"What does that mean? Do I have AIDS?"

"Well, that's why we're bringing you in, because you need to have additional test to confirm the presence of the HIV antibody."

Crystal didn't know whether to cry or scream. The air felt like it had been sucked out of the room. How could this have happened? Had Marcus really done this to her? There were so many questions running through her mind. Yolanda's words began to replay in her head like a bad song. "Make sure you're using protection with Marcus because obviously he's not."

"I'm going to die," Crystal said, her voice, barely above a whisper.

"Thirty years ago, that may have been the case. Now you can live a healthy regular life as long as you take your meds. This isn't the death sentence it used to be. I'm going to refer you to a doctor who specializes in HIV because further testing needs to be done. Again Crystal, I'm sorry about all of this, but if the test does confirm you do indeed have HIV, please remember there is life after testing positive for HIV."

Crystal hadn't heard a word Rachel had said after being diagnosed with HIV. The room began to feel as if it was closing in on her, and she was positive that she wasn't breathing at a normal rate. She had to get out of there, and fast. "I have to get out of here. I just can't deal with this now. I'll call the office to get the referral." Crystal grabbed her purse and was at the door in one swift move.

"There's one more thing Crystal. We're going to need you to give the names of your partners that you may have exposed. We have to notify them in order to prevent the spreading of the disease."

Without a word Crystal grabbed a posted note and a pen from the desk and wrote down Marcus's first and last name along with his phone number. Crystal handed the paper to Rachel. "There's only one person whom I've slept with and it's the same person that exposed me. I'm sure the list you'll get from him will be much longer."

Chapter 13

Crystal laid still on her couch as she stared at the ceiling fan going round and round. She had cried non-stop since receiving the news. She knew there was no way she would be able to return to work in that state. Everyone would have so many questions. Questions she herself couldn't answer. She was thankful that Aisha was at a friend's house and that she had time to process the news.

A part of her didn't believe that this could really be happening to her. She didn't feel like she had HIV, but she didn't know what HIV felt like in the first place. Her life had changed in a matter of minutes. There were so many feelings running through her body that she couldn't pinpoint it down to one specific sentiment.

She'd been betrayed, by someone she thought she was going to marry. She'd sacrificed her livelihood, her relationship with her children, and her self-respect all in the name of love. She truly believed that if she gave all of herself to Marcus, he would have no choice but to give her what she truly desired, which was to be his wife. The only thing he managed to give her was an overdrawn bank account, a broken heart, and now a fatal disease. She couldn't help but to think; was this punishment for the lifestyle she'd lived?

Knock. Knock. Knock.

Crystal turned to the front door wondering who could be at the door. Her girls were gone and she wasn't expecting any visitors. She hoped if she stayed quiet, they would go away.

Knock. Knock. Knock.

"There goes wishful thinking," Crystal thought aloud. Pulling herself off the couch, she dragged herself to the door. Looking through the peephole, she saw Yolanda standing with her hand on her hip. Crystal knew she had to open the door now because Yolanda wasn't going away. Since Crystal hadn't parked in the garage, Yolanda knew she was home.

Crystal swung the door open, and in marched Yolanda.

"I happened to see your car when I was driving by and decided to check on you. Is everything okay? Shouldn't you be at work?"

Crystal couldn't even pretend with her friend. She didn't try to hide her face or to wipe her streaming tears.

"Crystal, what's wrong?"

All Crystal had the strength to do was allow her body to collapse to the floor. "I'm going to die...I'm going to die."

"You're not making sense. What do you mean, you're going to die? Let me help you off the floor."

Yolanda helped Crystal off of the floor and onto a chair. "Are you sick, Crystal?"

"You were right, Yolanda. If I would have listened to you, I wouldn't be in this predicament."

"You're scaring me. I can't help you if you won't tell me what's going on."

"He gave me HIV."

Crystal couldn't believe that at thirty-seven years of age she was actually having this conversation. She wasn't the type of woman that slept around…she only slept with the man she was seeing. True enough he was married, but she only kept one partner at a time.

"What?"

"Yolanda, I'm HIV positive. Marcus gave me HIV." Crystal cradled her legs and cried like a baby.

"That damn Marcus … I'm so sorry, Crystal. I promise I'm here for you."

"Go ahead and say it."

"Say what?"

"I told you so. You had been telling me from day one to leave Marcus alone, and I just wouldn't listen."

"You know I wouldn't kick you when you're down. Everything is going to be okay. HIV isn't the death sentence that it used to be. You can still live a long healthy life if you take your medicine."

"Ha. That's exactly what the doctor said. It sounds good, but all I can do is keep envisioning myself being sick with twenty empty pill bottle's sitting in front of me."

"Get that out of your head because it doesn't have to be like that."

"Who's going to want me now? And the girls? How am I going to tell my girls?"

Crystal welcomed the hug that Yolanda engulfed her in.

"You'll have plenty of time to focus on your love life, and you'll know when it will be the right time to tell Lesley and Aisha. For now, let's just focus on getting your mind right and keeping you healthy."

"I'm not letting him get away with this. He has to pay for what he's done."

"Please don't do anything foolish. I promise you won't win."
"I'm HIV positive… I don't win either way.

Chapter 14

Crystal didn't sleep well at all, but she knew she couldn't afford to miss another day at work. That's the very reason why she sat at her desk trying to focus on the work in front of her. She had been at work for two hours already and had accomplished absolutely nothing. Crystal hadn't even worn any makeup, which was something she hadn't done in years. She figured, what's the use? Nobody would want her, so she might as well make herself less desirable.

"Crystal I just want to commend you on the awesome job you did with the blood drive."

Crystal hadn't heard Mrs. Parsons walk up, but she was truly glad to hear the friendly voice. "I really appreciate that, Mrs. Parsons."

"What's going on, Crystal? That fire you usually have in your eyes is gone."

"The better question is what isn't going on?"

"That bad?"

Crystal gave Mrs. Parsons a knowing look.

"I'm a great listener," said Mrs. Parsons as she took a seat next to Crystal's desk.

Crystal wasn't keen on telling her business to strangers, but Mrs. Parsons always showed her so much love. It was a love she had never experienced from her own mother. Crystal longed for that kind of love, but she had come to the conclusion that Essie didn't know how to give it.

"Whatever you tell me is between us. I hope you know that."

"I know…it's just so much and I don't know where to begin."

"Start from the beginning, child."

Before Crystal knew it the waterworks had started all over again. She really didn't want to do this at the office, but she was thankful the office was empty at the time. "Aisha is pregnant, and the love of my life betrayed me in the worst possible way. On top of that, my finances are a wreck. I don't know how to fix any of this."

"It's God's job to fix it, but you have to release it to him first. There's a lesson in everything you're going through. It's your job to learn it."

"You make it sound so easy."

"That's because it is. Aisha is a good girl; she made a mistake like we all do. Make sure you don't forget to show her the same grace that God has shown you so many times." Mrs. Parsons grabbed some tissues off of Crystal's desk and handed them to her. "Wipe your face just in case someone walks in. As far as your financial troubles goes, is it self-inflicted?"

Wiping the tears from her face all Crystal could do was nod. She couldn't even look Mrs. Parsons in the eyes.

"Well, I'm sure if you change the decisions that you make going forward, you can prevent this from happening, again. Now, as far as this love of your life, do you think the relationship is worth saving?

"Absolutely not. He crossed every line imaginable. The worst part about it all is that I still love him, but I want to get revenge so bad."

Mrs. Parsons gave Crystal the warmest look as she squeezed her hand. There was so much sincerity in her eyes.

"Don't ever beat yourself up for loving somebody. It only becomes a problem when you love them more than you love yourself. When I was dating my husband Edward, all those years ago, he called himself messing around with another woman while we were together. Lord knows I loved Edward's dirty drawers and he knew it too. So he figured that I would stay while he played games."

"I can't even see Mr. Parsons trying to be a player."

"Oh, you met him after the Lord had gotten a hold of him." Mrs. Parsons laughed.

"So what happened?" Crystal asked while she leaned in to get the rest of the story."

"Well, I had to show him that I refused to play second to any woman. If I wasn't enough for him I just had to move on. And that's exactly what I did."

"What made him come to his senses?"

"He couldn't handle the fact that I had moved on. I was being courted by another man, had finished college, and had landed my first teaching job. He couldn't handle the fact that I kept living without him. Then the word got out that my new man had proposed."

"I would have never guessed your life was such a soap opera."

"You live as long as I have and you'll experience more things than you could ever imagine."

"Why didn't you marry the other man?"

"Carl was nice enough, but I knew he wasn't the one for me. My heart belonged to Edward, but I couldn't let him think it was okay to treat me any kind of way."

"Wow, Mrs. Parsons. I would have never guessed."

"I said all of that to say this, sometimes living is the best way to get revenge. Strive for the best in everything you do and by doing so they'll learn that they didn't break you. I'm going to let you get back to work, but I'm here if you need me."

Crystal gave Mrs. Parsons the biggest hug ever to show her appreciation. She felt the best she had since she had gotten the news. "Thank you so much for taking the time to talk with me. You really help put things in perspective."

Chapter 15

Three weeks had passed since the talk Crystal had with Mrs. Parsons. The advice she'd received was priceless. Crystal definitely had experienced her share of bad days, but she refused to stop living because things had gotten tough.

Crystal and Aisha sat at the dining room table, eating the first home-cooked meal she'd cooked in a long time. Sure it was only breakfast, but it was a step in the right direction. The breakfast pork-chops, smothered potatoes, scrambled cheese eggs, and toast had the house smelling like her grandmother's kitchen.

Crystal had come to accept that the baby would be arriving soon and decided to take the time to start talking to Aisha about her future. Crystal had also just picked up her first round of prescriptions. Her doctor explained that taking the medication was vital and would be the only way to prevent her HIV status from turning into full-blown AIDS. The medication was very powerful and had the capacity to make patients sick in the beginning of treatment. Crystal wasn't sure about the complete impact the medicine would have on her body, but she wanted to enjoy one home-cooked meal before she found out.

"Just because you're about to be a mom, Aisha, I still expect you to keep your grades up. College is mandatory at this point. This baby is your responsibility."

"Yes, ma'am."

Crystal could still tell that Aisha hadn't completely come to grips about being pregnant, but she was happy that Aisha was at least willing to discuss it.

"I'm going to help you in every way I can; don't ever think you're alone. Do you understand me?"

"Yes."

"Go ahead and finish your food and get ready for school. I have to finish getting ready for work."

Just as Crystal cleared her dishes off the table, she could hear her cellphone ringing in her bedroom. Dashing to the phone, so the caller wouldn't hang up, Crystal cursed herself when she saw the name that appeared on the screen. Marcus had called her again. He'd called all day, every day for the past week. Crystal was pretty sure he'd been contacted about her HIV status and he wanted answers. This was his entire fault, and Crystal wasn't ready to talk to him. She knew she needed to, but today was just not the day. Sending the call straight to voicemail, she finished getting ready for work.

———

Crystal stayed in a daze for most of her ride to work. She hadn't discussed her HIV status with her girls yet. She knew that wasn't something that she could keep a secret from them for too much longer. They deserved to know that much. The problem was there was never a good time to deliver that kind of news. Lesley wasn't even living at home, and Crystal surely didn't want to stress Aisha out since she was pregnant.

Honnnnnnnnnnk!

Crystal had been so deep in thought that she'd hadn't realized the traffic light had turned green, but the angry drivers behind her had no problem letting her know how they felt. There was a time when Crystal would have gotten with the best of them and given them a few choice words right back. Now, things like that didn't matter anymore. Her life had changed drastically in the matter of seconds. Arguing over frivolous things just weren't worth it.

Before Crystal knew it she had pulled into her parking space at the church. She said a silent prayer that the Lord would give her the strength to get through the day. Crystal always arrived at the office about thirty minutes earlier than everyone else to make a pot of coffee and to be able to drink it in peace and quiet. Which is why she was so surprised to see Pastor Davis's car already there.

Crystal didn't expect the dark hallway after unlocking the door to the employee entrance. If Pastor Davis was already there, all the lights should be turned on. Crystal hit every light switch in her path as she made her way to the office. She wasn't all prepared for what she saw when she turned on the light to her office. There Pastor Davis lay, fully dressed in yesterday's clothes, fast asleep on the leather couch in the waiting area.

"Pastor Davis? Pastor Davis."

"Hmm?", was all he managed to say while shielding his eyes from the light.

Crystal didn't know what to do, but she couldn't let the other employees see him like this. "Pastor Davis, you have to get up before the other employees get here."

With those words Pastor Davis popped right up. "What time is it?"

"It's seven-thirty. You better get yourself together before any one else arrives."

Crystal could read the embarrassment all over Pastor Davis's face. He could barely look at her. It really hurt her to see her Pastor like this. Things had to be really tough between him and his wife if he was sleeping at the church. Not wanting to address the real problem and make him feel worse, Crystal began to carry on like this never happened. She understood all to well the place he was in.

"Pastor, I'm going to make a fresh pot of coffee. You go get yourself freshened up." Crystal placed her purse on her desk and headed to the kitchen. Crystal knew putting on a pot of coffee only took a few minutes, but she didn't want to go back into the office until Pastor Davis had cleaned himself up. She took the time to straighten up the kitchen a little and browse through a magazine while the coffee brewed.

By the time Crystal made her way back into the office, Pastor Davis was no longer on the couch and she could hear him moving around in his office.

"Thank you, Lord." She didn't need anymore awkward moments between them. Crystal sat down at her desk and turned her computer on. At five minutes until eight, Pastor Davis stepped out of his office looking like the Pastor Davis she was used to. He did look a little weary in his eyes, but life always managed to have that effect on people from time to time.

"Crystal, thanks for looking out. I really appreciate the way you handled this entire situation."

"It's no problem at all; things happen."

"This is true. Let me take you to lunch to show my gratitude."

"You don't have to do that."

"I know I don't have to, but I insist. I could use the company. As you can see, I've been dining alone here lately."

"Alright, Pastor."

"Good. Let's shoot for twelve-thirty."

"I'll be ready."

Chapter 16

Crystal snacked on the chips and salsa while Pastor Davis finished up his phone call. They had decided on Mexican food since there was a Mexican restaurant about twenty minutes from the church. It was nothing but a hole in a wall, but it was the real deal. Crystal hated Americanized Mexican food. If it wasn't authentic, then she didn't want it.

"I'm sorry about that, Crystal. I needed to handle that matter before the day got away from me."

"You're fine. As I said before, you didn't owe me lunch. I only did what I would hope somebody would do for me."

"I'm just showing my gratitude."

Pastor Davis sat in the booth across from Crystal and laid his napkin on his lap before digging into the chips and salsa. "How did you find this place? If you drive too fast you'll miss it."

Crystal had to cover her mouth while laughing, so no food would fly out of her mouth. "I actually found it by accident, and

I've been hooked ever since. I eat here at least twice a month. I would eat here more, but I try to watch my figure.

"You look just fine. I don't understand why women fuss so much about their weight."

"When you look good you feel good."

"I guess it's safe to say you feel good all the time?"

Crystal knew she was blushing because her cheeks became instantly warm. "I feel good most of the time." His comment really made Crystal consider her health. Could she really be sick? Physically she felt great.

"I didn't mean to embarrass you, just stating the obvious. Let's go ahead and order so we can get back to work."

Crystal answered by looking over her menu. She couldn't help but wonder if Pastor Davis could be her last chance to be a first lady and to have love.

———

Crystal sat on her couch with tears in her eyes from laughing as she listened to Judge Judy catch yet another defendant in a lie. "I don't know why they try that woman. They know she doesn't play."

"Mom, I can't concentrate on my homework with all that laughing."

"Girl, you shouldn't be in the living room doing your homework anyway. You know I don't play that. Go to your room and finish your homework. Yolanda will be over shortly anyway, and I need talk to her."

Knock. Knock. Knock.

"Perfect timing; Aisha open the door for your Aunt Yolanda before you go to your room."

"Yes, ma'am."

Crystal watched as Aisha dragged herself from the coffee table and waddled to the front door. When did she begin waddling? I look at her everyday, Crystal thought to herself. She couldn't believe how much Aisha's belly had grown in such a short period of time. "Don't forget you have a doctor's appointment next week."

"I won't. I'm a little excited since we're going to find out what I'm having."

Crystal was glad that Aisha's back was turned because she didn't want her to see how hard she rolled her eyes. Crystal couldn't deny that she couldn't wait to meet her grandchild, but she still wasn't at all excited about her daughter being a teenage mom.

"Hey, Aunt Yolanda."

"Wow. Look at you. That belly is really getting out there," Yolanda said.

"I know."

"How are you feeling?"

"I'm feeling okay."

"You let me know if you need anything."

"Yes, ma'am. Momma's in the living room."

Crystal waited for Yolanda to sit down before she opened the flood gates on all the tea she had to spill.

"Crystal, what was so important that you couldn't tell me over the phone?"

"Why did I get to work this morning and find Pastor Davis sleep on the couch in the waiting area?"

"Wait a minute. What?"

Crystal sat up to finish telling the story. "You heard me right. Pastor Davis is in the doghouse. I told you there are problems in his marriage."

Crystal watched Yolanda's eyebrows furrow as if she was thinking of the best way to respond.

"Why do you sound so excited?"

"I think God is giving me one last chance."

"A chance for what?"

"To become a wife and a first lady. You know he'll give you the desires of your heart if you're right with him."

"First of all, the Bible says to "Delight in the Lord, and he will give you the desires of your heart." God isn't going to put you in line with an already married man. Please don't be one of those Christians that twist the words in the Bible to make it work for them."

Crystal felt herself grow irritated, but she didn't let it show. After all she'd been through, Crystal thought Yolanda would be overjoyed for her happiness.

"Yolanda, I have no intentions on trying to make a move while Pastor Davis is married. I learned a lot from the Marcus situation. If Pastor Davis and his wife are having problems, God may be opening a door for me is all I'm trying to say."

"They're having problems, which most marriages do. They're not divorced."

"You always know how to find the negative in everything."

"That's not true. You just never want to hear the truth unless it's beneficial to you. I won't be a pretend friend and not be truthful with you."

"Whatever."

"Crystal, don't be like that. You know what I'm saying is true."

"I'm sure you have other things to do; it's probably best that you get going."

Crystal read the shock on Yolanda's face. Never had Crystal

put Yolanda out of her house. Crystal stood with her arms crossed as Yolanda rose from the couch.

"I've always had your back, and I take your backlash even though I'm just trying to help. But if you keep pushing me away…"

"It's best you leave so I don't say anything I'll regret."

"Do me this one favor, before you go professing your love to Pastor Davis. Make sure he knows your status."

Crystal had no clap back for Yolanda. Her comment had stung Crystal to the core. As hard as she tried to forget, she couldn't run from HIV.

Chapter 17

Crystal sat at the dining room table researching support groups from her laptop. It had been two months since her diagnosis and she still hadn't told her family. Yolanda was the only person who knew. Since they weren't on speaking terms, Crystal had no one to confide in. Yolanda had always been her person, and she missed her friend like crazy. Crystal's doctor had suggested joining a support group to help her with the emotional roller coaster she'd been riding. Never in her life did she think she would have to join a HIV/AIDS support group. Life had truly served her lemons, and she honestly didn't believe there was enough sugar in the world to make things sweet again.

Crystal's research was cut short with the sound of Lesley's voice. She hurriedly closed the laptop and went to the living room.

"Grandma, she doesn't want me here, why are you making me come back?"

"You're always welcome at my home, but it's time that you and your mother put this feud behind you. If too much time passes by, it allows pain to turn into anger and then resentment. You two have had plenty of time to cool off."

Crystal didn't have the strength to fight this battle. After seeing Essie, she knew a battle wasn't far behind.

"She needs to be here with you, so I'm telling you like I told her, get over it," Essie exclaimed.

"Essie, I do agree with you, but right now isn't a good time for all the extra drama." Crystal honestly missed having Lesley home. She definitely wanted to spend as much time as possible with her children, especially since she didn't know how much time she had left.

"I'm not leaving until there's a resolution between you two. You never want to deal with anything when it comes to your children."

Crystal stared at her mother. She realized the shenanigans between them had to end. She felt it would be best if Lesley wasn't around for this come-to-Jesus moment with her mother. Crystal felt it best to make her leave.

"Lesley, take my car and go pick up Aisha from school. Here's some money for you guys to grab something to eat. Give me and your grandmother a little time to talk."

Lesley grabbed the keys from the counter and left without saying a word. Crystal was thankful that Lesley obliged without an argument because Crystal needed all her energy for Essie.

Crystal patted the cushion next to her, signaling Essie to come have a seat. Crystal allowed her eyes to roam over Essie, from the crown of her head to the soles of her feet. She hated and loved this woman with the same intensity. This wasn't how a mother-daughter relationship should be, and if she wasn't careful she and Lesley would repeat the same cycle.

"Crystal, I don't have time for your mess, and I'm not giving you any more money until you pay me back what you already owe me."

Crystal laughed at her mother's defiance. She and her mother were truly two peas in a pod. They both jumped to conclusions and neither one of them liked to accept fault. In their world, everything revolved around them.

"About two months ago, I received the worst news of my life. I've been asking myself over and over again, how did I get to this point? Now, I won't blame you for all my life's misfortunes, but you had a great effect on some of the decisions."

"How?"

Crystal raised her hand towards her mother letting her know that she wasn't finished talking. "You're going to listen to me whether you want to or not. You're always putting me down about being such a bad mother. Have you ever asked yourself where my bad parenting skills came from? Somehow you've managed to block out all the bad things that you've done to me."

Essie had begun fidgeting in her seat. Crystal knew the conversation made Essie uneasy, but Crystal no longer cared. She had grown tired of tip-toeing around the subject.

"Did you forget that your boyfriend raped me? Do you remember, Essie? You couldn't convince him to leave his wife, and you used me as bait. You threw me to him like a rag doll. How could you?"

"Crystal, I'm not going to waste time replaying the past. You can't keep using that as an excuse for the mistakes you've made in your life."

Attempting to leave, Essie rose from the couch. Crystal wasn't having it and pulled her back down. "You're going to listen. And you're right, I can't keep using my past as an excuse, but you're going to take partial ownership for who I am today. You let him take my virginity. I wasn't even thinking about boys, and you let him take something so special away from me.

"Then I found out I was pregnant with Lesley, and you wouldn't even let me have an abortion. I lost my scholarship because of your selfishness. You really thought if I kept your boyfriend's baby he would make you first lady. But instead he left us and never looked back. I've never been able to bring myself to tell Lesley who her father really was. Tell me this, Momma, when you're bashing me to my kids do you ever tell them what you did?"

"All I can say is I'm sorry Crystal. I made a mistake, but it's time for you to move on."

"Move on! That one decision that you made for me changed my entire life! I've always questioned my worth. I have held on to this secret like my life depended on it since I was sixteen. I truly believed no one could really love me if my own mother would allow such a thing to happen."

"I'm so sorry. I don't know what else you want me to say," Essie spoke between sobs.

"I've let men take advantage of me, use me, and disrespect me time and time again. Now, I understand why Grandmother wanted me to know who I was and my worth. She wanted me to see past all my scars. Unfortunately, it took finding out I'm HIV positive to see my worth and discover how much bitterness has been rooted inside of me all these years."

"Momma, were you ever going to tell me who my daddy was?"

Shock decorated Crystal and Essie's face. They were so deep in their conversation, they hadn't heard Lesley come back in the house.

"Baby, let me explain."

"There's nothing to explain. My father is a rapist, which is why you treat me like you do. I'm a constant reminder of your pain. Grandma, you allowed all this to happen?"

Crystal rose and went to Lesley, but Lesley only pushed her away.

"Stay away from me. I don't even know who you two are anymore. And when were you going to tell me and Aisha that you have HIV? We deserved to know that."

"Baby, I never meant for you to find out this way." Crystal said.

I'm getting out of here. I can't deal with you two hypocrites right now."

"Watch your mouth! I'm still your grandmother and Crystal is still your mother! And you will respect us!"

"Respect! What about the lack of respect that you've shown me? You know what? Y'all are just some tired, wore-out, wanna-be first ladies. Your voice glorifies God's name, but the way you live your life shames Him. I'm going to go get Aisha. Don't worry, I'll make sure I catch her up.

Crystal and Essie watched as Lesley left and slammed the door behind her.

"I see what you mean about her being too grown for her own good. I don't know what's gotten into her."

Crystal couldn't believe Essie. "We're what have gotten into her. She just found out the truth about her father. How do you expect her to react?"

"She still needs to show respect. I don't care who's right or wrong."

"I'm not going to ignore her feelings like you did mine. She's right, a part of me has always resented her because of who her father is, but that wasn't her fault. I have to make things right with her. I refuse to have the kind of relationship with Lesley as I have with you. Starting today, if you can't treat me with respect, you're no longer welcome in my life. I will keep my girls away from you if I have to."

Crystal could see Essie fuming, but things had to change. If cutting Essie out of her life was the only way to do it, then so be it.

"I guess since you're sick you've finally gained morals?"

"You call it morals; I call it knowing my worth. I hate with every part of me that it took HIV to be the reason I opened my eyes. But they're open now, and your negativity is something I refuse to tolerate anymore."

Chapter 18

Crystal chuckled to herself as she read the message board on New Hope's website. There were messages, that some of the church members had left regarding last week's service. A lot of the older members couldn't look past the old-school church. The new style of music wasn't sitting right with them, and they weren't holding back. Crystal honestly didn't understand the big deal. The new music never took away from the word of God; it only had a different sound. Crystal read one more message before she got back to work, and it looked as if she'd saved the best for last. @GodFirst wrote:

Pastor Davis:

God never intended for such foolishness to be in his house. This church is going straight to hell if this devil's music isn't removed from the church.

Crystal almost hollered with laughter. She couldn't contain herself. She loved when messages got straight to the point. "Well, tell us how you really feel, @GodFirst."

Crystal carried on so loudly with her laugher that Pastor Davis came out of his office.

"I'm guessing you're reading the hate mail on the message board."

"Yes, Pastor. New Hope is going straight to hell if we don't change the music back to the old school."

Pastor Davis shook his head as he walked behind Crystal.

"Do you want me to respond?"

"No, it's no use. Some people are so set in their ways, it does no good trying to reason with them."

"Also Pastor, I'll be leaving in the next thirty minutes or so to take Aisha to the doctor. I'm just waiting on her to get here from school."

Crystal turned her chair around so she and Pastor Davis would face each other. She knew it wasn't right to feel this comfortable being this close with someone else's husband. She had promised herself that if things progressed with Pastor Davis it wouldn't be from her efforts. She would let God lead their union.

"How is Miss Aisha?"

"She's very pregnant. We find out what she's having today."

"And how are you dealing with it all? This can't be easy on you, either."

"I have my moments, but ready or not, this baby is coming." Crystal rose from her seat, putting her and Pastor Davis kissing-distance from each other. The brief pause between them let Crystal know that Pastor Davis wanted to kiss her.

"Momma?"

Crystal turned to see Aisha and Rodney standing in the doorway. Crystal had wondered how long they had been there. Although nothing had happened, it was obvious what was about to.

"How are you doing, Miss Aisha," Pastor Davis managed to say.
"Fine."

Crystal heard the irritation in Aisha's voice and, she could see the hurt in her eyes. She noticed Rodney had not said a word. He didn't need too though; his stiff body language said it all.

"Aisha, I'll see you next time around," Rodney said as he turned to leave.

"I'm going to get back to work and let you and Aisha get out of here."

"All right, Pastor. Aisha go ahead and have a seat while I finish up a few things."

Crystal watched Aisha roll her eyes as she plopped down on the couch. Any other time she would have addressed it, but she didn't want to make an already-awkward scene more uncomfortable.

———

Crystal sat in the corner of the examination room while she watched Dr. Holt, Aisha's OB-GYN, examine Aisha. Dr. Holt had just squeezed the blue gel on Aisha's belly, so she could do the sonogram. Crystal had watched Aisha's mood lighten as they made their way to the doctor's office in anticipation of discovering whether the baby was a boy or a girl. She hadn't admitted it to Aisha or anyone else, but she was pretty excited herself to find out the sex of the baby.

"The baby looks good and has a very strong heartbeat. This baby has long legs. He may just be a basketball player," said Dr. Holt.

"Did you say he? Am I having a boy?" Aisha couldn't contain her excitement.

"By the looks of this sonogram, you're having a boy. Congratulations, Aisha," Dr. Holt said as she took a napkin and wiped the remaining gel off of Aisha's belly."

"Momma, you're going to have a grandson."

"That's what I hear. I'm glad about it too. We have enough women in our family."

"Aisha, if you don't have any questions, I'll let you get dressed, so you two can get out of here."

"No, ma'am. I'm good."

"Well, I'll see you in about a month. Take care."

"See you later, Dr. Holt, and thanks again for giving such excellent care to my daughter."

"I wouldn't have it any other way."

Aisha waited for Dr. Holt to leave the room before she got up from the examination table. "Mom, can we have a gender reveal party?"

"A gender what?"

"A gender reveal party...It's a party where everyone comes together to find out the gender of the baby. Games are played to guess the sex of the baby. Food and drinks are served too."

"How is that any different from a baby shower?"

"No one has to bring gifts to a gender reveal. It's just a celebration for the expecting parents."

"I'm so out of the loop with these things. It's obvious that I haven't had a baby in my house for quite sometime."

"Is that a yes?"

"I don't care, Aisha. But it can't be anything too big because we'll be having a baby shower in the next month or two."

"Yes, ma'am. Thanks."

"Hurry up and finish getting dressed. I'm going to schedule your next appointment."

"All right."

Chapter 19

Crystal pulled the car into the grocery store parking lot. She listened to Aisha ramble on and on about the baby. Aisha had become a little chatter box since they had left the doctor's office. She kept throwing out different baby names. Crystal had to admit some of the names were cute, but some were just down right hideous.

"How about Joseph, Jackson or Malachi...Do you like any of those names?"

"I do, but what about this baby's father? I've tried to be patient and give you time, but you're yet to bring him up. You didn't make this baby on your own, and he is just as responsible for this child as you are."

Crystal parked the car as she waited on Aisha's response. Her bringing up the baby's father had brought Aisha's chatter to a halt. Crystal didn't want to upset her daughter, but this conversation was long overdue. "So who is he?"

"He doesn't matter. I'll take care of my baby without him."

"You didn't make this baby without him. Where did you meet this boy? Does he go to your school?"

"Yes."

"What does he have to say about all this?"

Crystal turned towards her daughter and waited on her response.

"He doesn't want anything to do with me or the baby," Aisha said through sobs. "As soon as I told him that I was pregnant, he changed. He told me the baby isn't his, but that's not true, Momma. He's the only person I've ever been with."

Crystal's heart broke into a million pieces to see her baby in so much pain. She herself understood the pain all too well. The only thing she knew to do was to wrap her arms around her child so Aisha would know that her mom had her back. A gesture she wished Essie would have done a million times over when she was in this position.

"It's going to be okay. Let the tears flow. I'll find out who his parents are and we'll get to the bottom of this. Okay?"

Aisha only nodded as she wiped away her tears.

Crystal's phone began to ring, and she cursed herself internally when she saw Marcus's name. She still hadn't spoken with him since she'd seen him with the other woman. That was water underneath the bridge. She knew he had probably been contacted since she given his name at the donation center. Although she never wanted to talk to him again, she knew she couldn't avoid him forever. She also knew that she couldn't talk to him right now with Aisha being in shambles. Sending the call to voicemail, Crystal tossed the phone into her purse.

"Did he give it to you, Ma?"

Crystal had hoped Aisha didn't see who had called. She wasn't at all prepared for that question, but Aisha deserved the truth.

"Yes."

"How sick are you?"

"I'm actually not sick at all. I found out very early. If I take my meds, I should be just fine."

Crystal watched Aisha's facial expression change. She knew she wanted to ask her something else but didn't know how to.

"What's on your mind, Aisha?"

"What about Pastor Davis?"

That question caused Crystal to gasp. She had no idea how to answer that question. She could always throw the "I'm grown" card and tell her to stay in a child's place, but where had that gotten her? Essie had done the same thing to her as a child, and Crystal had hated it. She had never been able to communicate whole-heartedly with her mother. So for her to do the same thing and expect a different result was insane. It was time to break this cycle.

"Pastor Davis is just my boss and a very good friend, nothing more."

"But you like him... I can tell."

"Aisha..."

"Why don't you like Mr. Rodney? He's a really good man."

"What do you know about a good man?"

"I know Mr. Rodney really likes you."

"I'll keep that in mind. Let's grab some dinner, and we'll continue this conversation later."

Chapter 20

Crystal arrived at the church a little earlier than usual. Just in case Pastor Davis had needed to sleep in the church again, she wanted to make sure she woke him in enough time. She didn't see his car there, so she figured he and first lady must have reconciled.

After she entered the church, she began her ritual of making sure all the lights were on in the building. After she put her purse down at her desk, she headed to the breakroom to start a fresh pot of coffee. She was a little caught off guard when she bumped into Rodney on the way to the breakroom.

"I'm sorry, Rodney. Good morning."

"Morning."

Crystal was taken aback by Rodney's shortness. He had never been short with her. Matter of fact, she looked forward to seeing him because he always managed to put a smile on her face no matter what mood she was in. Even the happiest person had their days, and Rodney was no exception. Thinking maybe she could reverse the roles, she tried lifting his spirits instead.

"How's that arm? Is it still sore from that big needle?"

By this time Rodney was facing the microwave while he warmed his breakfast.

"It's fine."

"Rodney, are you okay? What's the problem? You don't seem like yourself."

Crystal heard Rodney mumble, but she couldn't make out what he said.

"What did you say?"

"I said, 'My problem is you.'"

"Me? What did I do?"

"Don't worry about it."

"You brought it up, so I'm going to worry about it. And can you please look at me? I don't want to talk to your back."

Turning, Rodney looked at Crystal. And for the first time she really saw him. She took in all his features: peanut-butter-brown skin, brown almond-shaped eyes, thick eyebrows, and full lips. Rodney was truly a handsome man. His uniform fitted him nicely over his sculpted body. All this had been staring Crystal in the face and she never saw it.

"You don't know a good man when it's staring in your face. You would rather go for the dogs like Powers."

"Where is all this coming from?"

"When I first saw you, your beauty took my breath away. I asked around about you, and no one had anything good to say about you, except that you were pretty. I decided to put all the rumors aside and get to know you for myself. I'm glad I did because I learned you're not a bad person. You just make really bad decision about men."

Crystal hadn't realized she was crying until she felt the tears stream down her face. Rodney's words were comforting and painful. She had heard the rumors being said about her and knew a lot of the employees didn't care for her. To know that Rodney was willing to put rumors to the side and get to know her, meant the world to her. On top of everything, she had hurt one of the few people in her life that had her back.

"I'm sorry. I wasn't trying to make you cry," Rodney said as he handed Crystal a napkin off of the counter.

"I broke up with Marcus. I finally realized he was only using me."

"But now you have a new target. What's the use of changing men if you're not willing to change your pattern? I know I'm not a preacher and have people hanging onto my every word, but I would have treated you like queen. You would have felt like a 'first lady' without ever stepping foot in a pulpit, but you refused to see past what you wanted."

"I'm so sorry for hurting you, and I know you would have been good to me. But my circumstances have changed and I could never be the woman you need me to be."

"Good morning," Pastor Davis said as he came into the breakroom.

"Morning, Pastor," said Rodney.

"I thought the coffee would be ready by now," Pastor Davis said to Crystal.

"My apologies, Pastor. Time got away from me. I'll put a pot on now." Crystal said.

"I'll leave you two be. Have a good day."

Crystal watched Rodney as he grabbed his food and left the breakroom. She hated that they didn't get to finish their conversation because she didn't know where they stood. She only hoped that her being truthful with him wouldn't ruin their friendship.

The day was almost over and Crystal hadn't seen Rodney since that morning. Every time the door to the office opened, she prayed it would be him walking through. Rodney always found a reason to come visit her. There was no doubt that he was still upset with her.

She would have to focus on that later. Since she had a little down time, she finalized the plans for Aisha's gender reveal party. It was less than a week away, and Crystal wanted to make it special for her. Even with this being a small gathering, there were so many things to think about. She had managed to talk to the baby's father's parents, and they assured Crystal that they would be at the gender reveal party with their son in tow. Crystal wasn't the least surprised when they told her they knew nothing about their son having a baby on the way. Aisha was a little upset when Crystal told her that they would be coming, but she explained to her it wasn't about her wants any more. The baby deserved to know both sides of his family and Crystal was going to make sure he did.

Pastor Davis popped his head through the door. "Crystal, will you come to my office for a minute?"

"I'll be right there."

Other than during lunch, Crystal hadn't seen Pastor Davis all day. Whatever he had been working on had him completely focused. After straightening out her navy-blue pants-suit, Crystal headed to Pastor Davis's office.

"Yes, sir."

"Please have a seat."

Crystal took a seat in the leather wingback chair that sat in front of Pastor Davis's desk. She didn't know what to make of this meeting. He was conducting it a bit too formally, for her, and she hoped she wasn't in trouble for any reason.

"Crystal, I know I've been calling on you a lot here lately. With everything going on in my personal life and trying to have the youth center built, you have been a saint. I couldn't have made it without you. Because of this I would like to offer you a raise."

Crystal didn't know if she was more excited about the much-needed raise or because Pastor Davis was recognizing her for all of her hard work. Either way she couldn't be more grateful.

"I don't know what to say. Thank you so much."

"Don't thank me just yet. Take a look at the increase and let me know what you think."

Pastor Davis handed Crystal a piece of paper. She took a second just to scan the page only hitting the main points. Then her eyes parked on the line that stated her salary would go from forty thousand a year to forty-eight thousand.

Crystal was all smiles. That was almost a ten-thousand-dollar-a-year jump. It would have taken a lifetime for her annual raises to ever reach this.

"Thank you so much, Pastor"

"No, thank you. Crystal. You have exceeded the bar we set for you, and this is just a little way to show my gratitude. I do need one more favor."

"Anything."

"Will you attend one more business dinner with me? It's just to finalize everything for the youth center."

"I'd be more than happy too."

"All right. Once I confirm a time, I'll let you know."

"That will work."

Chapter 21

Crystal sat in her car while she waited for Yolanda to come out of her house. It had been almost a month since she and her friend had their disagreement. Not being able to talk to her hadn't sat right with her. After receiving her good news, Yolanda was the first person she wanted to tell, so she put her pride to the side and called her. Besides, Crystal knew that if Yolanda wasn't at Aisha's gender reveal party, neither one of them would let her live it down.

Buzz. Buzz. Buzz.

Glancing at her phone, all Crystal could do is roll her eyes. Marcus was calling her yet again. She vowed to herself that if she could just make it through Aisha's gender reveal party she would call him so they could talk. Sending the call to voicemail, Crystal prayed he didn't call her before she had a chance to call him. Marcus wasn't a patient man at all. Ignoring his calls would only make matters worse. Looking up, she saw Yolanda headed towards her car. Crystal admired her friend for always being so chic. The black and white floral-one piece hugged Yolanda's body in all the right places. The blue blazer with matching heels only made the entire outfit pop.

"Hey, girl" Crystal blurted before Yolanda could get in her seat good.

"Hey, yourself."

"Before I start driving, I just want to clear the air. I'm sorry for the way I behaved the last time I saw you. You didn't deserve that. I was in such a bad space, and I didn't want to listen to reason. I know you've always had my best interest at heart, and I don't want to lose our friendship over my pride."

When Yolanda reached over and hugged Crystal, she thanked God for Yolanda's child-like heart. It was always so easy for her to forgive.

"I'm not going anywhere. Sometimes space is good even with the closest of friends. Just know that I'm never trying to hurt you. It's all love."

Crystal extended her hands towards Yolanda so they could play the same hand game Celie and Nettie played in the movie "The Color Purple". As if on cue, Yolanda extended her hand as well and they began to chant in unison, "Me and you, us never part Makidada. Me and you, us have one heart. Makidada." Crystal busted out laughing before they could finish the song.

"I love you, girl."

"I love you more. Now, enough with all this mushy stuff, let's go shopping for this party," Crystal said as she drove off.

———

Crystal and Yolanda tossed party decorations in the shopping basket as they browsed the isles of Party City. Crystal's cheeks were hurting from laughter. Lord knows she needed it.

"Now, tell me this good news you're so excited about."

Crystal smiled with pride as she thought about the unexpected blessing she'd received.

"Well, if you must know…"

"Girl, stop playing and tell me."

Yolanda's frustration caused Crystal to giggle.

"Okay. Okay. Pastor Davis called me into his office and gave me an eight-thousand-dollar raise. It was so unexpected. Lord knows I need every penny of it."

"Congratulations. It's well deserved and overdue. You work hard for New Hope."

"You're right. It's the best news I've gotten in a long time. With everything that's been going on, I'd begun to feel like God had forgotten me."

"No matter how low the valley may seem, God would never forget you. Don't ever forget that."

Crystal knew her friend was right, but with everything she'd been going through, she couldn't hear God's voice. How could she not think that he'd forgotten her? Not wanting anything to ruin her moment she shook away all the negative thoughts.

"I need your advice about something."

"What's up?"

"Do you remember Rodney, my friend from work?"

"You mean the very handsome, and more importantly, single Rodney? Yes, I do."

"Girl, you're a mess. Anyway, he likes me, but I don't feel the same way. I think I really hurt his feelings. How do I fix our friendship?"

Crystal and Yolanda made their way towards the checkout. Crystal knew her friend was thinking about the best way to respond without offending her by the way her eyebrows were frowned.

"Speak what's on your mind, Yolanda. I promise I can take it."

"I don't have anything bad to say. I'm more confused as to why you could never see Rodney in a romantic way. He seems like a really great guy."

Crystal inched her shopping basket closer to the cashier as she thought about Yolanda's question. She honestly didn't know why she could never see herself with Rodney.

"I don't know. The only thing that comes to mind is that he's not my type. He's not the type of man I could ever see myself with. I know you think I'm a fool, but it doesn't matter now, anyway. What man is going to want me now?"

"The same man that God has had in store for you all along. I would almost bet that's he's nothing like you imagined, but everything you need. God is just awesome like that."

"I can help the next person in line," the cashier sang.

"I pray you're right. Let me checkout so we can get out of here.

Chapter 22

Crystal sat in the lounge in the lobby of the Omni Hotel in downtown Dallas. She had never been inside the hotel, but she was instantly impressed when she entered. The lounge reminded her of an upscale nightclub in a movie. The contemporary furniture and the rich color schemes invited a warm feeling. She assumed the overly–nice staff probably had something to do with it as well. She'd only been waiting for fifteen minutes and had already been asked by three different employees if there was anything they could get her while she waited. She truly appreciated the hospitality, but she really wished that they would let her wait in peace.

Honestly, she had become irritated that Pastor Davis had her waiting this long. Come to find out that things hadn't gotten better between he and first lady, so instead of sleeping at the church, he'd opted to get a room. They'd met for their final business meeting for the youth center today, and Pastor Davis asked if she could meet him at the hotel since the restaurant where they were meeting the other pastors was downtown. Crystal didn't mind coming to meet him, but she didn't appreciate having to wait. She hoped becoming

Pastor's personal assistant wasn't chained to the raise she'd just received. On second thought, that wasn't the worst thing in the world; that would mean she'd get to spend more time with him and learn to understand him on a personal level.

She felt the tension leave her body as the elevator doors crawled open and Pastor Davis made his way towards her.

"I'm sorry to keep you waiting, I laid down to take a power nap and overslept."

Crystal waited for Pastor Davis to say something else, but he stood frozen with his eyes fixed on her. "Pastor Davis, is everything okay?"

"Excuse me for staring, Crystal, but you look absolutely stunning."

"Thank you, Pastor. We better get going; we're already running late."

"Well, let's be on our way."

That was the second compliment that Pastor Davis had given Crystal. Now, she couldn't help but wonder if this had simply been a compliment or was he actually flirting with her. She knew time would reveal all things.

———

Crystal sat at the dining table having what she thought was an out-of-body experience. She could hear Pastor Davis, Pastor McCullum, and Bishop Jackson talking, but she hadn't listened to a word they said. She couldn't believe how her life had changed so drastically. Who would want her now? And how soon do you tell someone that you're HIV positive?

"Crystal. Crystal."

"Hmm."

"We're going to be on our way, but it was a pleasure meeting you again," said Pastor McCullum.

"It's an honor to work with men as yourself who want to give back to the community," Crystal said. She knew she was laying it on thick, but she felt it was the least she could do since she hadn't been very present at the meeting. She shook the gentlemen's hands and watched them head toward the exit.

"Are you in a rush, Crystal, or would you like some dessert?"

"No, thank you."

"Is everything okay? You didn't say much through dinner."

"I apologize. I guess I'm a little tired, and I'm trying to mentally prepare myself for Aisha's gender reveal party tomorrow."

"Well, let's get you back to the hotel so you can be on your way."

"All right."

———

During the short ride back to the hotel, Crystal noticed that Pastor Davis's demeanor had change. He was more solemn, and she was sure it was because he missed his wife. Crystal knew all too well how to pretend like everything was okay, only to get alone and finally take the mask off. Pastor Davis had kept up the charade for as long as he could, but Crystal knew the view of the hotel brought him back to reality. Sensing his uneasiness, Crystal tried to give a word of encouragement.

"Pastor, no matter what, you're a good man, and don't ever forget that."

"I wish my wife could see it."

"I'm sure she does. Even us women let pride get in the way

sometimes. I better get going, I have a long day tomorrow," Crystal said as she waited for Pastor to finish parking his SUV.

"Yes, of course. Let me walk you to your car."

"That's not necessary. My car is only a few feet away."

"I was taught to be a gentleman at all times."

"At least I can't say chivalry is dead."

"Not at all, let's get you to your car."

Crystal used her remote to unlock her car and allowed Pastor Davis to open her car door. He extended his "We're just friends and I love the Lord" hug like he always did, but in that moment Crystal wanted more. Before Pastor Davis had a chance to pull back, Crystal kissed him. A part of her expected him to pull away, but when he didn't, Crystal laid her arms on his shoulders.

As they kissed, Crystal used her fingers to massage the nape of his neck. She inhaled his cologne. It wasn't the usual fragrance that he wore at the office. This was something else, something exotic. She didn't know the brand he was wearing, but the scent had become an aphrodisiac to her. She wanted him in the worst way. And by the way his hands explored her body, the feeling was mutual.

With each moment that passed, their kisses grew more passionate. When Pastor Davis slid his tongue between Crystal's lips, their tongues began to dance. Feeling herself lose control, Crystal thrust her pelvis against his. When she felt he'd grown in size, she knew they had to take their party to a more private setting.

"Let's go back to your room," Crystal whispered.

"Hmm?"

"We can go back to your room, so no one will see us."

Those were the wrong words to say because Crystal instantly felt Pastor Davis's body go rigid as he pulled away.

"What's wrong?"

"I can't do this?"

"Why not?"

"Because I love my wife."

"Then why did you kiss me back? I know you felt something between us. You can be honest with me."

"What just happened was a moment of weakness. I took vows with my wife before God... I plan on honoring those vows."

Crystal reached for Pastor Davis's hand, but he quickly pulled away.

"Pastor, you said yourself that your wife hasn't been happy with you for quite some time. But I'm here. I can be everything you need and more if you would just let me."

"My wife is the only woman for me, Crystal. Let me help you into your car, so we don't do anything that we'll regret."

Crystal felt like the wind had just been knocked out of her. Too embarrassed to speak, Crystal stepped aside and allowed Pastor Davis to open her car door. After she was completely in the car, Pastor Davis closed the door and walked towards the hotel. Crystal watched through tear-filled eyes, hoping that Pastor Davis would at least turn back around. Realizing he wasn't coming back for her, Crystal watched until Pastor Davis had disappeared into the hotel.

Chapter 23

Crystal sat on the edge of her bed, trying to pull herself together. It was Saturday and the day of Aisha's gender-reveal party. All Crystal wanted to do was lay in her bed with the covers pulled over her head. She'd robbed Peter to pay Paul to acquire her beautiful home and the things in it. She never had her own room growing up, so she promised when she got her own place she would live like a queen. Her home was supposed to be her place of peace, where sleep would come easy… but sleep hadn't come easy for her. The embarrassment she wore from Pastor Davis's rejection of her was overbearing. Now, she couldn't help but wonder if she would even have a job come Monday.

Knock. Knock. Knock.

Crystal knew that had to be Aisha. She knew her daughter was excited about the party, but the feelings weren't mutual.

"Come in."

"Good morning, Momma. Did you sleep in your clothes?"

"Yes. I was so tired I collapsed on the bed as soon as I made it home," Crystal lied.

The truth was that she'd cried so hard when she came home last night that she didn't have the energy to get undressed.

"Aunt Yolanda said she'd be over in an hour with the cake and to help cook the food. I already cleaned the house. Is it okay for me to start putting up the decorations?

"Have Lesley help you with the things that need to be hung because I don't want you to slip and fall."

"Yes ma'am."

Before Crystal knew it, Aisha had thrown her arms around her neck.

"Thank you, Momma. I know this isn't easy, but I appreciate you being there for me."

It took Crystal a few moments to return the hug. After everything that had happened to her, she'd begun shutting down her emotions, even with her children. She'd been functioning on autopilot, and she didn't know how to turn it off.

"I'll always have your back, no matter what. Now, go ahead and start decorating, so you can get dressed. I'll be out shortly after I get myself together."

———

Over and hour later, Crystal walked out of her bedroom, looking better than she felt. This would definitely be one of those days where she had to fake it until she made it. She would be meeting Aisha's baby's father and his parents and a few other people for the first time. Wanting to make a good impression, she wore a simple, sleeveless, form–fitting, black dress. The dress was plain enough, but once she added a gold statement necklace and her diamond-stud earrings, the outfit came to life. Since she knew she would be hosting and running around the house, she opted to wear sandals with a small heel.

Glancing at the clock on the wall, she realized she didn't have much time left to prepare her famous crab dip and tuna salad. Had she gotten out of bed after Aisha had left her room, she would have had time to spare. But the more she thought about the night before, getting out of the bed seemed like an impossible task.

Looking around, Crystal had to admit that the girls had really done an awesome job with the decorations. The colors blue and pink seemed to be in every inch of the living room. Aisha and Lesley hung a blanket of blue and pink balloons on the ceiling. Crystal couldn't help but think that if the girls had done all this for the gender reveal, they were going to pull out all the stops for the baby shower.

"Aisha, where's the hand mixer? I need to get the cupcakes whipped up, so they'll have time to cool," Yolanda said.

"Didn't you already bring the cake? Why do you need cupcakes?" Crystal said as she followed Yolanda and Aisha back to the kitchen.

"I just wanted to make sure we had enough," Yolanda said.

"Enough for who? Only a few people are coming. No more than ten," Crystal said.

Crystal turned to Aisha, waiting for her to confirm the number of guests. She conveniently had her face deep in the cabinet, pretending she couldn't find the mixer.

"Aisha," Crystal snapped.

"Yes, ma'am."

"How many guests are coming?"

"Well, a couple of Lesley's friends are coming too."

"How many?"

"Maybe twenty."

"Aisha, we agreed to something small. I didn't buy enough food for that many guests."

"Crystal, leave that child alone. I brought a few extra things, so we'll have plenty."

Crystal watched Yolanda take the mixer from Aisha and began dumping ingredients into the mixing bowl.

"Aisha, go get dressed," was all Crystal could say. It was taking everything in her not to go on a fussing rampage, but she didn't want to ruin Aisha's day.

Without a word, Aisha disappeared into the other room.

"I swear, Yolanda, you're going to have to stop spoiling them so much. They're rotten."

"I've been doing this all their lives, why stop now?" Yolanda said through a smile.

"When I send them home with you, I bet you change your tune."

"Excuse me while I turn this mixer on and tune you out."

All Crystal could do was laugh. Once again, Yolanda sensed Crystal's mood and had found a way to brighten it without ever asking a question.

Chapter 24

Crystal scanned the room and counted the number of guests. Aisha was dead on. Twenty people had shown up, and surprisingly everyone was on time, give or take ten minutes. She'd never attended a party with a majority of black people where everyone was on time. Well, that wasn't completely true about Aisha's baby's father and his parents. Aisha had failed to relay that the Lincoln family was white. Them being white hadn't bothered Crystal, but a heads up would have been nice. What if the food they prepared was too salty? She didn't know how true it was, but she had heard that white people didn't care for salty food.

Crystal now wondered if this be the reason why Aisha hadn't wanted to tell her about Christian. Crystal didn't even know that Aisha was attracted to white boys. If she had to be honest with herself, she didn't know Aisha was interested in boys at all. She had to admit that she'd lost so much valuable time with her kids because of Marcus. Nonetheless, Christian was a very handsome young man and seemed to be well mannered. Crystal could understand why Aisha had been attracted to him. He didn't say too much, but Crystal didn't know if it was because he was shy or just didn't want to be there. She didn't care one bit. The only thing she was concerned about was him being an active father in her grandbaby's life.

"Okay, everyone! It's time to reveal the baby's gender?" Yolanda announced.

Yolanda brought out the gender-reveal box and placed it between Aisha and Christian. Crystal noted that this was the first time Christian seemed to be interested.

"Nine people say it's a girl, and eleven people say it a boy. Does anyone want to change his or her vote before we open the box? Remember there will be prizes given to those that guessed correctly." Yolanda waited a moment before proceeding. "Going once, going twice... All right! Aisha and Christian, open the box."

"Do you want to open it?" Aisha asked Christian.

"No, you go ahead," Christian said as he used his foot to push the box in front of her.

Crystal watched excitedly as Aisha ripped off the pink and blue ribbons and slowly unfolded each flap of the box. The gender-reveal box was a good idea. Lesley did a great job decorating the box. The pink tutu and blue helmet were an added touch. When the last flap was folded back, the room erupted with applause when the blue balloons came flowing out the box.

"It's a boy!" Aisha yelled.

While all the congratulations and hugs were being circulated, Crystal decided to start cleaning up. That way she wouldn't have to do too much once everyone was gone.

"Ms. Long, Aisha is a lovely young lady. I apologize again for our son keeping us out of the loop. Had we known sooner, we would be more involved. I'm so excited we're about to have a grandson," said Mrs. Lincoln.

"No apologies needed. Aisha hid her pregnancy from me as well. My oldest daughter, Lesley, broke the news.

"Kids, I tell ya. Anyway, we're excited about welcoming her into our family."

"Welcoming her? You mean the baby, right?"

"Actually, I mean both. The kids will have to get married."

"Married? Aisha is only fifteen."

"Well, age didn't stop them from making this baby."

"They're not even old enough to work or live on their own."

"My husband and I wanted to talk to you about that. We were thinking that since we have the means, Aisha and the baby can move in with us once they're married."

Crystal could feel her blood boiling. She fought everything within herself to keep a cool head.

"Aisha will not be getting married anytime soon, and she definitely won't be moving in with you all."

"Ms. Long, we're only trying to help. Please don't get offended."

Knock. Knock. Knock.

Mrs. Lincoln didn't know that baby Jesus had just saved her with the knocks at the door.

"Mrs. Lincoln, please excuse me, I need to get the door."

Crystal took in long, deep breaths to calm herself. The person on the other side of the door didn't deserve the wrath that was brewing within her. Who Crystal saw when she opened that door caused the time to stop. Marcus stood there, towering over her with a demonic look in his eyes. She should have known that she couldn't ignore him forever. Marcus wasn't the type of man you ignored.

"Marcus what are you doing here?" Crystal could hear herself stuttering. She knew this meeting wasn't going to be good.

She tried to step outside the house and close the door behind her, but Marcus wasn't having it. With one move he'd pushed the door back open and her along with it.

"How could you do this to me, Crystal? I have a wife and kids."

"Marcus, now isn't the time. Keep your voice down."

"Keep my voice down. Are you serious? Oh no, sweetheart. If you're going to destroy my world, I'm about to return the favor."

Crystal knew there was no reasoning with Marcus at this point. He was a mad dog on the loose that couldn't be tamed until he sank his teeth into her.

"Marcus, please don't do this now. As you can see, we're having a party.

"Then this is the perfect time." Marcus said as he brushed past Crystal.

"Marcus, please." Crystal tried one more plea, but it was to no avail.

"You gave me HIV. Begging will not help you now!"

Instantly, the room grew quiet. She and Marcus had an audience. Her secret was out, and as embarrassed as she was, she felt worse for Aisha and Lesley. Now, their friends knew that she was HIV positive. The looks on their faces said they were thinking the same thing.

"Did you all hear that? This beautiful woman is HIV positive and she gave it to me."

Crystal didn't have the energy to argue against what he was saying. It wouldn't change the fact that she had HIV.

"Marcus, it's time for you to leave," Yolanda said as she made her way toward Marcus.

"I'm not leaving until I finish saying what I have to say."

"You've said enough. Now, I'm asking you to leave. Please don't make me call the police."

Crystal could tell Marcus had reservations about leaving, but she knew he didn't want any part of the police. Easing back toward the door, Marcus stopped in front of Crystal and whispered in her ear.

"This isn't over. I won't rest until I destroy your life just like you destroyed mine."

Chapter 25

Crystal dreaded the ride to work, and it wasn't because it was Monday traffic in Dallas. She hadn't spoken to Pastor Davis since the night they'd kissed, and she didn't know where they stood. She hadn't thought about it much since Marcus came and ruined Aisha's gender–reveal party.

Lesley and Aisha said they didn't blame her for what happened that night, but how could they not? Their world had been turned upside down because of her decisions. She wouldn't be able to forgive herself for that.

Crystal spent the remainder of the weekend trying to figure out how to make things right for everyone, but there was no resolution. God would have to be her refuge. After all the wrong she'd done, she was sure that He had turned from her as well. She didn't deserve grace, and she'd stop asking for it. The irony about it all was that she spent more time at church than anywhere else, but she still was so far from God.

After pulling into the church parking lot, she immediately knew that God's grace surely hadn't met her at work. Not only did she see Pastor Davis's car in the parking lot she'd seen Marcus's as well.

"What is he doing here?" Crystal asked herself. Remembering Marcus's words before he left her house gave her the answer. *I won't rest until I destroy your life; like you destroyed mine.*

Still trying to save face, Crystal threw her car in park, jumped out her car and began running to the church. She didn't want Pastor Davis to find out that she was HIV positive like this. He would think she had intended to give it to him, and that wasn't the case at all.

Busting through the office door, she could distinctively hear two men's voices coming from Pastor Davis's office. Crystal needed to catch her breath and get her bearing, but there was no time for that. She had to get to Pastor Davis before it was too late... if it wasn't too late already.

"I'm telling you Pastor Davis, she's no good for your congregation. Think of the other victims that will suffer."

"Pastor, please don't listen to him, it's not how it sounds," Crystal said as she burst in the room.

The two men turned towards her, and for only a few moments, a deadly silence fell over the room.

"Pastor Powers, thanks for filling me in, but I believe I can take it from here," said Pastor Davis.

Crystal watched Marcus rise from his chair wearing a mischievous smile. He didn't take his eyes off her until he'd left the room. She couldn't help but wonder if this torture was how he was coping with everything.

Pastor Davis waited until he heard the door shut before he spoke. "Have a seat."

Crystal slid in the chair in front of Pastor Davis's desk in one swift move. She felt like a child being scolded for misbehaving at school.

"Is it true?"

Crystal couldn't bring herself to lock Pastor Davis in the face. The shame she carried was unbearable. Man of God or not, he had the right to never want to forgive her again.

"Yes. I'm HIV positive, but Marcus gave it to me."

"Where you got it, doesn't matter. That night, had I let you come up to my hotel room...would I have been your next victim?"

Crystal felt the burn in her throat as she fought to hold back her tears. Trying to be strong had completely worn her out. Pretending she had it all together had cost her everything. She no longer cared who saw her in all her weakness and allowed her tears to fall.

She looked up for the first time ready to face Pastor Davis. Gone was the softness that she always saw in his eyes. His look was stoic.

"I never had any intentions to sleep with you. What happened the other night just happened. I just reacted; I didn't have time to think."

"You didn't have time or didn't want to?"

"I never meant to hurt you. You have to know that."

"I don't know what to think anymore, but I do have to agree with Marcus. You're no good for New Hope, and I'm going to have to let you go."

"Pastor, please, you just gave me a raise a week ago, and now you're taking my job away?" Crystal managed to say through sobs.

"You've left me no choice. Now, please gather your things and leave. Don't forget to leave the church's keys and your badge on the desk."

Crystal pulled herself from her seat and dragged herself to the door.

"I meant what I said when I told you that you're a good man. I hope you will find it in your heart to forgive me. Don't let my bad decisions change you."

"The rest of the staff will be here shortly. I'd would appreciate if you were gone by then."

Chapter 26

Crystal let the box drop to the ground as soon as she walked through the door. The loud thud caused her eyes to follow the sound. A few of her picture frames spilled out the box. A picture of Aisha, Lesley, and herself caught her attention. It was the church's annual picnic. The three of them looked so happy. It was a happiness Crystal didn't think she would ever experience again, but she wanted more for her children. Crystal understood all too well that life had its unforeseen circumstances, but Aisha and Lesley were just kids. She'd made their life more difficult than it had to be. She knew what she needed to do.

Crystal went to the back of her closet and found the all-white off-the shoulder gown she had hidden. No one knew about the dress, including Yolanda. She'd bought the dress on the whim one day while out and about running errands. She found it in one of her favorite boutiques at the Mockingbird Station in North Dallas. The dress was a steal and she couldn't pass it up. She held on to the dress as she waited for Marcus to give her the green light on their engagement. She'd always dreamed of a big wedding, but she was more than willing to elope or go to the courthouse if Marcus had only toyed with the thought of actually marrying her. Unfortunately, that day would never come, and this dress would now serve another purpose.

After spreading the dress out on the bed, Crystal laid her undergarments next to them. It was a matching nude and lace set. Crystal then went to the bathroom to run a bath. Wanting lots of bubbles, she added more than enough bubble bath. She pulled her hair into a bun and then slipped out of her clothes. Before stepping into the water, she examined herself from head to toe in her full-length mirror. Physically, she was gorgeous, but none of that mattered. It never did.

After easing her foot in the water to test the temperature, Crystal eased the rest of her body into the steaming hot water. The water was a bit warmer than she liked, but the liquid sauna felt good on her stiff body. She'd always been a fan of hot baths. It was her way of clearing her mind, something she desperately needed to do. She had to make peace with the decision she was about to make. Crystal allowed her body to sink a little deeper in the tub as she nodded off to sleep.

The cooling of the bath water was what woke Crystal from her slumber. Grabbing the bath towel, she wrapped it around her body and stepped out on the bathmat. She toweled herself dry as she made her way to the bedroom. Crystal took her time applying her Victoria's Secret "Love Spell" lotion to every inch of her body. After slipping on her dress, Crystal went back to the bathroom and put on her make up. She decided on a more natural look for a change, hoping to resemble a sleeping angel. Finally, she let her hair down and allowed her curls to fall around her face.

Glancing at her clock, she realized that it was already twelve-thirty. If she wanted her plan to work she needed to be done before the girls made it home from school, which was at four. Crystal went to her medicine cabinet and pulled out every pain medicine she owned, prescription and non-prescription. She knew she would have to pace herself in taking them all so she wouldn't throw them up. Taking all the pill bottles and grabbing a bottle of water, Crystal headed to her bedroom and began popping pills.

Knowing that this would take a while, she decided to write her girls a letter. She dreaded this part more than anything. These would be the last words she ever shared with her children. She could only hope they wouldn't hate her for doing it this way.

Dear Lesley and Aisha,

I want to apologize for being such a disappointment to you. Which is why I've decided to take my own life. You're better off with me in death than here with you. As a mother, it was my job to protect and nurture you. Instead, I put you in harm's way. Please know that I love you with all my heart and I never meant to hurt you. My insecurities gave men the permission to use me and treat me like I was worthy of less than God's best. I know I didn't do my best to teach you how to conduct yourselves like ladies. Please let my death be a lesson to you. Never sell yourself short for anybody or anything. If ever you feel less than one of God's princesses, let it go… whatever it may be.

I love you with all my heart in life, and death,
Momma

Crystal slid the letter into an envelope and wrote Lesley and Aisha's name on it and sat it on her nightstand. After taking the last few pills, Crystal laid across the bed and let death take its course.

Chapter 27

Crystal peeked through heavy eyelids as she tried to fight off the grogginess. She had no recollection of where she was. The bare white walls didn't help jog her memory in the least. It wasn't until she tried to use her hands to rub her eyes that she realized her arms had been restrained. This caused all the events up until that moment to come rushing back like a flood.

And the only thing left for her to do was to lie there and process it all. Tears seeped out of the corner of her eyes as she thought on how she had failed in everything she had ever attempted in life. How in the world she had failed in suicide, she would never truly know, but had to believe that God had to have played a major role in it. Her grandmother used to always tell her "God has the final say." Crystal knew she was living proof of that.

Crystal couldn't help but wonder what her grandmother would be thinking if she could see her now. She'd probably be turning over in her grave. Crystal had gotten so far away from her grandmother's teachings that she didn't recognize herself. If she was ever going to get her life back in order, some serious changes had to be made.

"Ms. Long. I'm glad to see you're finally awake."

Crystal turned her head ever so slightly to find a nurse standing with a chart in her hand while wearing a big smile. The nametag she was wearing said "Susan" in dark letters.

Crystal went to speak, but her throat was so dry she couldn't raise her voice over a whisper if she wanted to. What she did know is that her breath smelled and tasted horrible. She couldn't remember the last time she'd brushed her teeth, but she was pretty sure it hadn't been since she'd been in the crazy house. What did they think she was going to do with a toothbrush, shank another patient?

"Crystal, there's someone here to see you. Are you up for visitors?"

Crystal nodded her head even though she didn't really want to see anybody.

"I'm going to take your restraints off; if you try anything, they're going right back on and there won't be any visitations today. Are we understood?"

Crystal managed to mouth the word, "Yes."

As if that was the magic word, that needed to be spoken, the two male techs that had restrained Crystal before came marching in the room. All they needed were black suits and glasses, and they would look just like the men from the movie "Men in Black".

What they didn't know was that Crystal didn't have any more fight left in her. They would get no resistance out of her.

"Who's here?"

"I believe she said her name was Yolanda. I'm sure you're still a little drowsy from the medicine I gave you earlier, so on the count of three we're going to help you stand to your feet. Okay?"

"Yes."

"Here we go. One... two ...three and up you go."

It took Crystal a few seconds before she got her bearings, but eventually she could stand on her own.

When they arrived at the visitor's room, Crystal could feel her heart begin to race. This would be the first time she would have to face someone since her suicide attempt. She was embarrassed that she'd even tried to commit suicide and even more embarrassed that she had failed at the attempt.

"You seem a little hesitant, Ms. Long. Are you sure you're ready for visitors?"

"I can't hide forever," Crystal managed to say.

"Very well."

Crystal walked through the doorway to find Yolanda sitting at a table.

Yolanda didn't say a word, she just walked over to Crystal and threw her arms around her. Yolanda hugged Crystal so tightly, she was cutting off her circulation, but Crystal didn't say one word.

"You have fifteen minutes. I'll come back and give you a two-minute warning."

Realizing they were on a clock, both women sat down.

"You look good. Yolanda." Crystal couldn't even look Yolanda in her eyes.

"Crystal, you gave us a scare out of this world. We almost lost you. I don't know what I would have done if you...if you had...I can't even bring myself to say the word. Why?"

"After everything I'd done, I truly felt your lives would be better without me. How are my girls?"

"Both are worried to death, but you would be proud of Lesley. She has really stepped up. I think with what happened to you and

135

then with Aisha having to be rushed to the hospital because of her blood pressure, well, it really pushed Lesley to put things in perspective. Her doctor has Aisha on strict bed rest. Her blood pressure has to be taken every hour, on the hour."

"Lord. How's the baby?"

"They're both doing fine. But Christian's mother is really pressing for Aisha and the baby to come live with them. Especially, after everything that has happened."

"I never thought I would hear these words come out of my mouth, but that may not be the worst idea."

"Crystal, how can you say that?"

"How can I not? Look at my life; it's completely out of control."

Crystal knew Yolanda didn't like what she was saying and was trying to come up with another solution. "They can come live with me."

"Yolanda, I can't ask you to do that."

"But you'll send them with strangers? Come on, Crystal. You're talking like..."

"A mad woman?"

"That's not what I was going to say."

Crystal tried smoothing her hair and clothes hoping that would make her look less crazy.

"Why didn't Essie come? She should have been the first to come see me."

"I can't answer that, but she does send her love."

"Her love? Even after everything that's happened, she still can't bring herself to be there for me like a mother should. Do you know how bad that hurts? I don't even know why this still hurts me. If nothing else, Essie has always been consistent in who she is."

"Crystal I can't even begin to imagine how you must feel, but it's time to move forward. God has given you a second chance. Make it count."

"How do I move forward? I can't make this right. Marcus has made it his business to destroy my life."

"It's time to let go, and let God."

Crystal hadn't realized she was crying until Yolanda passed her some tissues that she'd dug out of her purse.

"That sounds so easy. I've been trying to do it on my own since..." Crystal couldn't bring herself to say the words.

"Say it, Crystal. It's time to release that pain."

"I can't." The thought of Crystal reliving that dreadful day caused her entire body to cringe. The ache in her heart she'd felt at sixteen was making its presence felt.

"Yes, you can."

"He raped me in his office and then told my momma that I asked for it. I begged her to believe me, but she turned her back on me. I was only sixteen. She was supposed to be my protector!"

Crystal hadn't realized that she was yelling until Nurse Susan came running through the door.

"It's okay; she's just getting things off of her chest," said Yolanda.

"You have five minutes left," Nurse Susan said as she walked back out the door.

"I lost two things that day: my virginity and my mom. Somewhere along the way, I figured if I married a pastor and became a first lady it would fix all my problems."

Crystal fidgeted in her chair realizing how naïve she'd been all these years.

"I forced myself not to think about that day; that's the only way I knew to survive."

"Surviving is all you've been doing. God wants you to live… live in Him. Let Him be your ally. He'll never turn on you. Now, your doctor told me you should be released in the next three days. Let your release be your new beginning."

Crystal thought about Yolanda's words. She'd had grown up in church her entire life and never completely opened herself up to God. She'd been straddling the fence for years, too afraid to allow herself to be vulnerable, especially with God.

"Okay, ladies, visiting hours are over," Nurse Susan said as she entered the room.

Crystal and Yolanda rose from their seats and hugged one last time.

"In three days Crystal, you get a fresh start. Keep that in mind to help you deal with the dark moments," Yolanda whispered in Crystal's ear.

Chapter 28

Six Months Later

Crystal sat in her bedroom, burping her grandson, Christian Michael Lincoln Junior. This little boy had stolen everyone's heart. If she didn't stop holding him so much, he was going to be spoiled rotten. She just couldn't help it, he was so precious. It actually was the birth of her grandson that had given her that added push to make it through each day.

She would be lying to say she didn't experience bad days. Days where she couldn't conceive the thought of forgiving herself, but as her counselor had often told her, those days were to be expected. Healing was necessary, but never easy.

Her girls were a great support system, especially Lesley, who was now working a part-time job and taking classes at a community college. She wanted to be a doctor and told Crystal every day that she was going to find a cure for HIV. God had a mysterious way of making the worst situations work for our good. Her child had done a three-sixty, and Crystal couldn't be more grateful.

Aisha was also doing well. She'd managed to maintain her four point GPA. Her girls were going to do great things. Crystal wasn't the least surprised that Aisha was an excellent mother. Her patience had worn thin with baby Christian's other grandparents, though. They were still trying to force the two kids to get married. Aisha didn't even want to be with the boy. Crystal hoped she wouldn't have to lose any heaven points by putting the Lincoln's in their place behind her child or grandchild.

She and Essie were even taking steps in the right direction. True enough, they had a big uphill battle to climb, but they both were trying. The two had to learn each other all over again, so the two treaded the water carefully when communicating with one another. Crystal refused to accept anything but respect from Essie. She'd already let Essie know that the failure to do so would be an automatic dismissal from her life.

All things being said, things were good for Crystal. She'd managed to find another job as the executive assistant for a CEO of a mortgage company. She'd decided not to seek employment through churches anymore. It had gotten her into too much trouble.

She'd also made amends with Pastor Davis and his wife. They were really good people, and she had no right trying to break up their home. She decided to find a new church home so she and the girls would have a fresh start. Pastor Davis said that it wasn't necessary, but Crystal believed it was for the best.

Crystal hadn't heard a peep from Marcus, but Yolanda said he'd been fired from Freewill because of all of his infidelity. Crystal had to find peace with him, whether he deserved it or not. She now understood that he was a part of her journey and she had to meet him in order to be healed. She'd never known a peace like she had now; she carried a grateful praise in heart. Her grandmother would be so proud. She had truly found her worth.

Knock. Knock. Knock.

"Aisha, get the door," Crystal called from her bedroom. Crystal didn't know who that could be because they weren't expecting any visitors. Crystal heard the door slam, but hadn't heard any voices. "Aisha who was that at the door?"

A few moments later Aisha walked into Crystal's room crying holding a letter in her hand.

"Aisha, what is wrong with you? Why are you crying and who was at the door?"

"The Lincolns are trying to take my baby away. They want full custody."

"What! Let me see that letter." Crystal scanned the letter and couldn't believe her eyes. The Lincolns had indeed filed a motion seeking full custody of baby Christian.

"Aisha, I'm not going to let them take your baby away, okay? I'll find a lawyer first thing in the morning."

Crystal shook her head in disbelief. If it wasn't one thing it was another in her life.

The End

www.ingramcontent.com/pod-product-compliance
Lightning Source LLC
Chambersburg PA
CBHW020402130626
46549CB00006B/2404